# Collection of Kisses

G.S. Steele

Printed in the Canada
First Printing, 2014
ISBN 0993661300
ISBN 978-0-9936613-0-3
Northern Phoenix Press northernphoenixpublishing@gmail.com

May you find out something that you didn't know?

# 1

*I*'m just not sure how too start this thing. How's that for the first line in a book? Does it grab your attention? Does it hold you rapt enough to want to read some more? Obviously because you are still here. That in and of itself is an accomplishment of sorts I suppose. See I am a bit of a perfectionist Dear Reader. I want to get it right.

One hundred years from now, if, man survives, I want the people who are left to know and remember my book. Maybe I am being grandiose. What I mean I want is an "it was a best of times, it was the worst of times" sort of thing. A quotable beginning and here I have gone and started my book with "I'm just not sure how to start this thing".

I really am surprised you have stayed with me this far. Well guess what? I am calling in a mulligan. Yep! A good old fashioned do over. If I want to make sure that the introduction to my book is memorable, I am just going to have to start over so here goes......introduction......... Take two.

In the beginning, once upon a time, in a land far far away. When I was thirteen years old, on a dark and stormy night, it was the best of times and it was the worst of times.

Ok I know what you are thinking and guess what? Fuck you! I don't care what you think. I have not seen another living person for....... ohhhh....must be at least sixty days now. So, look, if that's how I want to start my book. That is how I am going to start my book. Nothing you could say will change my mind. If I want to use a combination of the greatest introductions of all time, I will. Besides, you are still here aren't you? Though you may roll your eyes at the audacity of using that introduction, you do have to admit it is way better than "I don't know how to start this thing".

Since you have come this far and I don't want to disappoint you. I feel I should warn you, I should be straight forward, open and up front with you from here on. Right from the beginning. If you are looking for one of those tales full of blood and guts, beyond human heroics and a happy ending....... Weellll.......You may be disappointed. I don't even know how it all started. I have my suspicions; we'll just save those until we know each other better.

This will not be one of those tales where the hero rises up from the depths to attain the pinnacle and through some duplicitous trick of fate loses everything. Reaching the bottom he pulls himself up by his bootstraps and reaches even higher heights. This won't be some crazy adventure tale.

Mostly the tale I have to tell is my own. So if you have reached this point and have decided to put these pages down........well, you aren't going to hurt my feelings none. I will understand. For you see I am going to continue on anyways. While I wait I don't have much else to do so I will write. I will let you know how I came to be here. Probably we will talk about my dreams. Mostly we will talk about me.

My goal Dear Reader is to capture a moment and preserve it for you. Have you ever watched the sunset with someone you love? The second before the sun disappears and the glorious pink sky is trapped in her beautiful eyes. That second I want to capture. I hope to find it in my ramblings, the proverbial diamond in the rough.

So I think I have done my part by letting you know what you are in for. I have been as straight forward as I can. I don't want to hear any bitching from you at the end. You have your chance here and now. I can only hope that you decide to join me. I will give you a moment to think about it and I will be waiting for you on the next page.........

# 2

God....the day it began was so incredibly mundane. We did not have a meteor shower, comet, or some other celestial event. I have not heard some long drawn out tale (though my tale may be at times) of some overworked, overtired, lab assistant letting some biological agent escape from a secret government facility. No radioactive or toxic leaks. No seven trumpets sounding, seven seals breaking, or lords leaping for that matter. This would have heralded the rapture and Armageddon, promised in the book of revelation. No one could have predicted that the beginning of the end would be a whimper, not a BANG!

For those of us who survived, assuming I am not the last. It will be one of those days we will always remember. I had heard my parents talk of remembering where they were when John F Kennedy was assassinated. I can remember my teacher wheeling in a TV on a cart when Challenger blew up. The confused and garbled reports that filled the radio. We thought they were a joke in bad taste, early on the morning of September 11th 2001.

January 23rd 2013 will be one of those days. Only more so. The day the dead rose up to claim their due. The day human civilization died. It sounds so dramatic but really it was a plain old ordinary day. I awoke to my alarm at the same time that I always wake up. I went through my usual morning routine. I showered trimmed my beard and brushed my teeth. I had my usual breakfast of champions, 2 coffees, and 2 cigarettes.

A cold wet nose nudging my leg was the understood signal. It was time for me to grab the leash and take the pup for a walk. It was cold, as Artan leapt and bounded through the field behind the house. You could almost cut each of my exhalations with a knife.

After I caught my breath. I should really stop smoking. I called him in and answered a few emails. Then I called her real quick just to tell her that I loved her and to hear the smile in her voice. I did some paperwork. Then I called Sebastian to make sure we were still on for a movie later. After that I went to put some gas in the truck. As you can tell just a plain old ordinary day.

Before we go too much further, let me first thank you. I am glad you have decided to come with me even just this far. Even if it is only a trial run and you are reserving judgement for some future point in time. I do appreciate the fact that you have given me the benefit of the doubt.

Since we are going to be spending so much time together, let me introduce myself. I mean why stay for the story if the teller is a stranger right? So.....hi, my name is Greg. I would shake your hand; my dad taught me the importance of a firm handshake when you meet someone. Clearly though that is not possible. I just want you to know that I wish I could honour that social convention.

So like I said "my name is Greg". Near as I can figure I will be 36 years old soon. I was born July $7^{th}$ 1977, at 7 in the morning and I weighed 7 pounds 7 ounces. This means I have 7 7's in my birthday.

Like I have also pointed out before this will mostly be my tale, and for the most part it may only interest me. So if you need to re evaluate your decision to stay I will be ok with it. If I had to compare this tale to something I would compare it to a fart in a crowded room. A few people will walk away, a few people will be too polite to say what they really think, one will point out the obvious crap and everyone likes their own brand.

Now I am not saying that what I am writing here would win me a Pulitzer Prize (even if it still existed). Clearly though I am going to like my own tale that I am spinning. I truly hope that you do too. Mostly I am writing this tale for me. Putting this pencil to paper will help me stave of insanity, and help me figure out how and why I survived, when so many didn't. A roundabout way to determine fates plans for me, by gazing back over previously woven threads.

My hope for you whoever you are is that you are able to find the similarities in your own tale. I also hope I get to hear it. You will have to bear with me Dear Reader. I have oft been accused of being long winded and at times my tales seem to veer off on a unrelated tangent but eventually more often than not I will get back to whatever seemingly important to me point I was making.

Earlier when I mentioned that I had 7 7's in my birthday I bet you thought to yourself "Wow, he must be lucky". I guess in a lot of ways I have been lucky in my life. As I sit here alone writing these pages and the flames of my campfire dance and flicker I acutely feel her loss and I don't feel so lucky. I just feel empty, like something is missing. Don't get me wrong I survived right? So that is a good thing. I am sure she survived too and so this loneliness is only temporary while I wait. If you met her you would not question whether or not I was lucky you would know. More about her as we go along I am sure. Right. Now let us get back to day one.

# 3

*I*t was just after filling up my truck with gas, that I first began to feel like something weird might just be going on. As I was pulling away from the pumps, I could have sworn that I saw a middle aged woman pounce on this guy filling up his car and bite a gushing hole out of his neck. I am sure I saw her cheeks puff up with arterial spray as her teeth sank into him, like a chipmunk that is running from the birdfeeder to his hidey hole.

At the time I dismissed the whole thing. I turned up my radio and fortuitously I heard "Wake up it's time to die!" blast thru my speakers. An omen if ever there was one. Why was I able to so easily put this strange attack out of my head? Well like most of my generation I had been inundated with so many images of horror including the zombie apocalypse. I would like to add here for the record, having lived through a zombie apocalypse, not near as much fun or as easy as "Shawn of the Dead" made it look. Suffice to say not an experience I would wish on anybody.

You would be safe in saying that I grew up on zombies. I watched the films; I did all the quizzes on face book. My friends and I took the time to discuss our various survival strategies. I read Brook's "Zombie Survival Guide". In fact I even read "How to Properly Feed and Train Your Zombie". In case you are wondering even the most simple of tricks like sit and roll over seem to be beyond a zombies capabilities so you can avoid that book, it is a great fun read though.

I am sure now that you can see how I was able to dismiss this attack as at least my overactive imagination or at most another aberrant story like that guy down in Florida, who attacked and tried to eat another guy's face and for some strange reason, it took a slew of bullets to bring him down. Stories, comments and posts circulated the net for days about the impending zombie apocalypse. For a further example how about the strange encounter of two men in Germany, You may have heard of them? They met on a cannibalism web site, one for his own screwy reasons decided he wanted to be eaten. The other for equally if not more so screwy reasons wanted to eat someone, so they chatted for a bit and made a dinner date to share a sausage. Ha Ha Ha, it has been said that I have a dark sense of humour. I grew up on Monty Python and The Three Stooges does that explain it? Enough said eh.

So ya these two German gentlemen, it is a true story, seriously. How could you make this stuff up? There is a famous quote by Mark Twain that says "the truth is stranger than fiction". I am sure he could not have even conceived of such a story. They made a movie about it. It is called "Grimm Love". This was the backdrop of my mind that day and the world in which we lived in.

You might or might not be surprised how often in my daily life the subject of the zombie apocalypse actually came up. We would discuss the pros and the cons of various survival strategies around the dinner table. Drill the plans into each others heads over cigarettes in the garage until each man knew his roles and responsibilities. Sure there were lots of doubters who mocked us for having a plan. Our universal response was to take them off the list of people to rescue. The depth of our planning is what allowed me to survive thus far. The reason I can wait here. Be prepared I was a boy scout after all.

It was no big deal that some mocked us, really I understand why for the most part. We used to live in a world of terrorist bombings, North Korean missile tests, unemployment, starvation and people regularly voting liberal. Clearly there were more prevalent and relevant horrors for people to consider than the eminent walking dead.

# 4

*I* have had a bit of a cold, so it has been a couple of days since I have put pencil to paper. My daily routine here is repetitive to the point of monotony. Mostly I eat, sleep, work out, and I try to remember. Writing it all down helps. I don't want to leave you with the impression that, that is all that I do. I have a security system that I regularly check. This is not some elaborate electronic jobby, but rather a system of empty beer cans strung around the perimeter of my campsite. I also hunt and fish for my food. As you may well see I love the hunt. Sometimes I go into town for canned goods and sundries.

I like to avoid town though. Inevitably I will see one or more hulking shambling husk of humanity and by this time let me tell you the novelty has worn off. I am not so complacent as to put myself at risk, but I am no longer terrified either just resigned to this world. It amazes me how readily you can accept a new reality.

Lately, maybe because I have been thinking so much about my own life, I have been finding that as I dispatch a zombie with a severed brain stem, I wonder who they were, what they were like, how they lived, in the time before zombies. My pet term is BZE (before the zombie era). It may have been only a couple of months since the outbreak but there is a clear delineation and the world is definitely irrevocably changed.

Mostly I just sit by my fire and wait. Someone told me a long time ago that a man alone with just his thoughts is in bad company. So I have started to write out my life. With the hope that you Dear Reader will find these pages and lets be honest, that you will enjoy this tale of me. Don't believe for a minute that I am not writing this for you, as much as to stave off insanity Dear Reader. It is really just a bonus that by doing this I get to preserve me. Though I have been accused (sometime justly) of making stupid decisions. I am not a stupid man. So I know that insanity is really inevitable. As I sit here waiting for her, piece by piece I will lose my mind.

So that half seen flash in the trees. That feeling from the base of your spine.....creeping, getting stronger, of being watched, DON'T!!!..... For god's sake don't turn around and look. The half starved, half naked, bedraggled man partially hidden just beyond the tree line watching you with eyes drowned in fear and struggling curiosity. Unable to come out to greet you, who's lost all the trappings of being a civilized man. That is only one of my possible outcomes. I sure hope I can stave it off by putting pencil to paper.

Mostly I wait, that is how I spend my time, waiting. I have spent a good portion of my life waiting. After all, all hunting from a stand or blind is a waiting game. So I am pretty good at it. In fact some of my earliest memories are of waiting. Seriously, maybe that seems strange, but it is what I remember.

The house I grew up in had 3 really big windows in the front. Not the kind that stick out. What are they called?......Bay windows......French windows, doesn't matter I suppose, just 3 big picture windows.

As a young boy I would sit amongst the plants and terrariums and pretend to be in a forest or a jungle while I waited for my dad to come home from work. I can clearly see myself staring out the window, mesmerized by the passing cars, counting the trucks. Waiting for the red one that would stop in front of the house, in my minds eyes I can see Dad getting out of the truck. He would reach into the back to grab his battered grey lunch box and stainless steel thermos. Even now I can remember the excitement building with this daily ritual.

As dad would start up the driveway, the jungles and forest would be forgotten and I would race to the back door to greet him. First the creak of the screen door, then the handle turns. Me rocking on my heels with quite poorly contained excitement. The door finally opening and I leap from the landing into his arms.

Daddy caught me always and swinging me around his head he would ask, "How's my little man today?" The answer depended on the day. To that little boy the most dreaded words in the English language were "just you wait until your father gets home." This would change the daily ritual by mixing in apprehension with the excitement. I wasn't afraid of my Dad. I just didn't want to disappoint him. Over the years I am sure I provided him with plenty of opportunity to be disappointed. I often wonder what he would think of the man I have become.

One gift that my dad gave to me that has stayed with me for the duration of my life is a love of words. As a young boy, just after my bath but before I said my prayers. Dad and I would sit against the backdrop of the most garish of black and gold couches and he would read me a bedtime story.

Each and every night my head would be filled with stories of knights and damsels and dragons, forest or barnyard animals that all got along and went on fantastic adventures. Just before bedtime was filled with, once upon a times and my cue for sleep, the words that invited the sandman were "and the moral of the story is". I could never get enough.

Even when I could read by myself, I would stay up long past my bedtime. Tracing my alarm clock up and down the pages, reading by the red digital read out.

Man.... I wish I had of had a tale to tell when there were still people around to hear it. Well I can't give up hope. Just because I haven't seen anyone for a while that doesn't mean anything. It would be easy to give up hope I suppose. Put this pencil down. Oh don't worry Dear Reader. I will consider your feelings, besides I still believe in the power of love and in happy endings.

# 5

So are you asking yourself yet, why you have even bothered to read this far? Some kid sitting in his living room by the front window, waiting for his dad to come home from work. It's not much of a hook is it? No sex, no violence, nothing that really sells.

Well when you picked up this tale (despite my warnings) I am sure you secretly hoped for, blood and guts, a cross country quest to save mankind from the waves of undead corpses. A ravenous zombie horde falling on a band of stragglers, like a pride of lions tearing apart a cape buffalo. Perhaps a memorable movie moment that is designed to make a young woman scream and nestle herself deep into her dates arms. The undead bursting through a plate glass window, gripping by the eye sockets and cracking the skull open like an

Easter surprise to get to the delicious brains hidden inside.

That stuff happened, for sure it did. I also recognize that if you are reading this, well, then you survived too. You have your own tale and you have seen enough gore and horror to last many lifetimes. My graphic descriptions can't help. You don't need me to point it out to you.

When I think back on it now I really am amazed, remember how that stuff used to sell? Books, movies, video games. I wasn't immune. I read, I watched, I played. In fact it would be safe to say I was a gore junkie. I loved a good or even a bad for that matter, horror movie. I wanted to be scared. I dared to be shocked.

Now as I sit here it seems almost sacrilegious to write about that stuff. I know I have defiantly gotten my fill.

So if that is what you are still hoping for, please, put these pages down. Even though I don't know you, I would hate to disappoint you. I have disappointed enough people in my life already. Now just before you throw down these pages, indulge me for a few more lines please. I don't want you to storm away without saying, where it applies, I will include the gore.

I would hate to see you leave now. I am just starting to get comfortable with you. So stay. Please. Mostly this tale will be far removed from the typical horror story. This tale could more aptly be called a romance and in places a dramatic tragedy.

At the risk of further alienating you while you get comfortable with the idea of reading a romance, I feel obliged to tell you that I have never read a romance novel and I have only seen a few romantic comedies. So my understanding of the genre is limited at best. So if you are a romance fan, well....... I will most likely leave you feeling unfulfilled.

I can only tell my tale the way I would tell any tale. Long winded and disjointed, sometimes saying things twice, just to make sure you understand and of course going off on an unrelated tangent every now and then. It may also get worse depending on my mind. Just saying.

# 6

We were talking about my dad weren't we? I would imagine that we will come back to him often since he figures so prominently in my life.

When I was a kid no matter what my activities were dad was there. He was my Sunday school teacher, my baseball coach, and my Cub Scout leader. Dad was our ride to the ski hill and from the youngest possible age I could be found at his heels learning his bush craft, from searching for wild horseradishes to tracking moose across a clear cut or in the boat spending a lazy summer afternoon catching fish. Even chores would be done side by side, from shovelling snow to kneeling next to him pulling up weeds in the vegetable garden. It was dad who tightened my skates or supervised our sliding down at Deadmans

Lake. Even when we were old enough to go on our own, dad would have the fire in the fireplace roaring when we got home and mom would have for us a steaming cup of hot chocolate.

Did your community have a Deadmans lake? A local legend, a beast in the forest, a haunted house or a Dogman perhaps? Most communities have something right? Maybe it is the old woman with a plethora of cats who lives up on the hill whom everyone is convinced is a witch.

Communities seem to be able to hold on to their ties to the supernatural long after science managed to kill religion.

In my hometown one of the local legends concerned a little swamp that we lovingly referred to as Deadmans Lake. The whispered tales of this cursed locale drifted down to our eagerly waiting ears. They hinted at chaos, destruction, death, and enough horror to hold our young attention spans raptly.

One day, depending on whom you asked, it was one hundred or two hundred years ago. One little boy we came across was convinced it was a thousand years ago. Let us go with the most common and realistic version here.

One day, one hundred years ago. A little boy (probably he was the same age as whatever little boy you were telling the story too) was playing down by the railway line. He was placing coins on the train tracks to add to his collection of flattened coins. The train completely unprepared for a coin on the tracks hit the coin full force. This jarring collision caused the train to derail into the swamp next to the tracks. The bottom of this swamp was a special type of quicksand that reached up and pulled the train down to the depths trapping all the hapless passengers (again estimates vary from tens to thousands). This fate left them condemned to roam the night wailing and bemoaning their curse, searching for other souls to join their lonely vigil.

Inevitably the story would end with a double warning. If ever you went down to play by the train tracks "they" would come and get you. Also if you were ever unlucky enough to be caught down there at midnight you would hear all the lost souls crying out for succour.

Let's be frank. None of us kids had ever been down there at midnight. We were all tucked safely into our beds by then. We all accepted this tale as absolute truth nonetheless and I don't have a single childhood memory of playing on or near the train tracks.

# 7

*A*round the time I was ten (really only a best guess) I remember Mr. Roberts was my teacher and that was grade five. So around the time I was ten, I decided for some reason, I really wish I could remember why. Obviously I was in trouble for something, maybe it was report card day. I was one of those kids; you know the ones, maybe one yourself, who was always being told about their potential quid pro quo if only I would apply myself. How I was bright but disruptive. It always led to lots of fighting in my house. When I was 22 or 23 a psychologist diagnosed me with Attention Deficit Disorder, as a kid though I was just considered bad.

Regardless of the reason, to avoid getting in trouble yet again, I decided it was time for me to set out on my own. I packed up everything I would need and with an assurance that only a ten year old boy can possess I pointed myself west.

I should add here that I was also "deeply" in love. She was exactly what I felt I needed. She was an older woman, as she was twelve, tall and blonde haired and attractive. On a moonless night she had kissed me in behind cabin 4 at bible camp the previous summer.

I'll be damned if I can remember her name right now....hmmmm...... Marcie, Marhyl, Mellissa (no but we will get to her). Michelle! Yep that's it Michelle. Her cousin Chris is the only guy I ever heard of who was hit by a pizza delivery truck, delivering pizzas to his own house. I digress, I warned you about the tangents Dear Reader.

I suppose even at ten years old the hopeless romantic in me was well on its way to being developed, even if it only included the abstract concepts of love, magical kisses, and happily ever after. In my defence though isn't that how these once upon stories are supposed to end? Once upon a time at summer camp has a fairy tale ring to it. A Princess kiss and even a big bad ogre (my dad and his belt). All the makings of a great story.

I am sure if you close your eyes you can picture this love struck prince setting out across the countryside to claim his true love, and to avoid the wrath of the ogre and live happily ever after.

I should add here that the next year if I remember correctly I was the victim of some other girl's version of grab a boy and kiss him in behind cabin 4. Charlene maybe?

Then I knew so little about women, I doubt I know much more now.

So try and picture it anyways, ten years old, with my backpack over my shoulder. I set out for my adventure filled life. One foot in front of the other, I walked through town and I had made it all the way to the cemetery, feeling really quite pleased with myself I must say, when my thoughts started to shift. The more I contemplated my adventure the more I realized that there would probably be people I would miss, I had my friends, and there was my dog and my mom and dad. Though I predicted they were going to give me hell. Surprisingly I decided that most of all I was going to miss my uncle Larry.

Now before I begin to tell you about Uncle Larry. I just want to say that even at this late juncture, if you want to stop reading here I won't hold it against you. I could understand if you feel disappointed. Not only has there been absolutely no blood and guts so far. On top of that the only romance has been a single kiss behind a cabin by a couple of kids at summer camp. I have to say really kind of a dismal start. It is my tale however and I will tell it like I want too. So if you decide to continue on with me, well........

# 8

So Uncle Larry was a very interesting, looking back in hindsight, if not odd individual. Too young for world war one, he went down to the train station in his hometown of Lindsay Ontario with his pack on his back and an inspired determination to make something of himself in his heart. Thinking back on this story now I can almost imagine this young lad standing out in front of the train station trying to figure out in which direction to head. Hitting upon the solution to his dilemma, he spit into the palms of his hands and upon clapping them together, promptly marched into the train station and bought a ticket in the direction the spit flew, west (really how could you make this stuff up).

This ticket brought him to the town of Richan Ontario about an hour north of Dryden Ontario.

Larry got himself a homestead next to a small lake and built himself a cottage. Trapping and making snowshoes out of birch and moose stomach leather which he sold for a dollar a pair. This is how he made his living and he spent most of his spare time repairing his cottage for it seems a couple of beavers had taken offence to Larry and were regularly felling trees onto it.

One thing that stuck with him and a story he told often was, during the 1930's, Larry would always check on his neighbours in the Richan area. On one such round he found an elderly couple froze to death with their arms wrapped around each other. This image would haunt him for the rest of his life and he would often mutter at the end of the tale "at least they died in love".

If you decide to measure a man by his deeds one story truly sums up the man that Larry was more than any other.

During the worst of the depression, Larry got it into his head that there must be an awful lot of children out there who wouldn't have any toys for Christmas. So he started in the spring spending his spare time making toy trucks and doll cradles out of birch. When winter began to hint that it would rapidly be approaching, he loaded up his gear and the toys he had made and he began his trek. Arriving on December 23$^{rd}$ like a true to life Santa Claus with his pack on his pack and on snowshoes he dropped his toys off at a Winnipeg orphanage. His little hike for the children was roughly 400 kilometres. Imagine on

Christmas morning all the happiness that arduous trek must have brought.

When World War two broke out and leather became a war material, even if it came from a moose stomach. Larry decided the snowshoes were not worth the hassle. He started making toys full time and he sold those for his meagre income for the rest of his life. After he passed away we found notebooks full of the names of children who had his toys, some lived as far away as France.

Larry came into my families' life quite by happenstance. My parents also from Lindsay moved to Dryden in 1971. On his trips into Dryden Larry would often stop at the Ontario Provincial Police station where my mother worked, having some common ground they became friends, though by this time Larry was 71 years old.

Despite the hour drive my family would make the trip a couple of times a year to go and visit "Uncle" Larry at his shack. Another couple of times a year Larry would join us for dinner when he happened to be in town. I grew up playing with Larry's toy trucks and my sister had one of his magnificent doll cradles.

The July previous to my once upon a time adventure, Larry had given to me a prototype for a new baseball bat he was working on. A birch core with copper piping over it and individual one inch rings of birch placed overtop, then hand lathed. That baseball bat stayed by my side until the zombies overran my truck and it was lost in the ensuing melee.

So I hope you can see why it made perfect sense to my ten year old brain that I should at least go and say goodbye before I walked off into the sunset to collect my happily ever after.

Armed with a much clearer plan now, I happily set out for "Uncle" Larry's shack. 25 years ago is a long time ago so I am not going to claim a perfect memory. I am not sure what possessed me but eventually I got the idea that if I stuck out my thumb I might just catch a lift. Seemed easier than walking, so that is exactly what I did.

I can almost hear you gasp Dear Reader. A helpless ten year old boy, hitchhiking!!!! Even to me it seems so crazy looking back on it now. Who knows who could have been out there? The world is full of stories of sickos', who kidnap, who rape, who torture, who murder. All I can say is I guess I grew up in a different time.

Needless to say someone stopped to pick me up. I really wish I could remember what believable story a ten year old boy could have told that man to convince him to drive me all the way to Richan, sure enough though he drove me out to 'Uncle" Larry's shack.

With a determination that only a ten year old boy on a quest can possess, I stomped up the driveway and rapped on the door. It sounded to my young ears like each knock was echoing throughout the cavernous shack. I can almost even now hear the shuffling footsteps. I catch myself mid-breath as the door creaks slowly open and the hulking shadowy form in the doorway gradually gives way to a wizened jovial old man.

Gathering me up in his arms he carried me through the workshop, into the side room that he slept and cooked in. To this day I connect the smell of freshly worked wood with safety and security. It is a truly comfortable scent for me. In fact now that I think about it, I wonder why nobody ever made a sawdust scented candle?

He sat me down on his bunk, put a steaming mug of tea in my hands and said "so chum what brings you out to see this old man?" Drawing up my shoulders and puffing out my chest I told him that I had come out to say goodbye. Once the words started to trickle out, it didn't take very long for my whole brilliant plan to burst forth into the open.

With a kindly chuckle hidden in his voice he suggested that I should stay and at least get a good nights sleep. Being able to see the wisdom in his words I agreed to stay but "only until morning".

He sat me on his knee and for the first time told me the tale of a boy not much older than myself buying a train ticket with spit on his hands.

At some point Larry must have called my parents because suddenly dad was standing in the doorway. I could have sworn if I didn't know how tough my dad was that he had tears in his eyes. The second I saw him I was overcome with homesickness and the desire to go home, I leapt into my Daddy's arms.

Something changed that day and it was the beginning of my separate relationship with Larry. Over the next few years it would not have been a strange sight to see an octogenarian and a small boy traipsing through the bush, practicing our moose calls, learning how to survive in the forest or hand feeding the whiskey jacks, as I write this I am flooded with memories. Most of them are for me alone, I will however share one with you Dear Reader.

Did you know that you could ride a wild moose? Not like paying for a camel or elephant ride at the zoo. Actually ride a wild, lives in the forest moose? No I bet you didn't. Well let me tell you how it is done and how we did it. First though promise me that you won't try this at home….. Ok good I believe you.

Even now, so many years later I can remember it so clearly. It was one of those late June days, beautiful, warm, with a faint breeze lightly rippling the water causing it to glisten as if it was seeded with thousands of diamonds. The perfect silence only interrupted by the odd bird call, and the sound of our paddles cutting through the water as we guided our canoe across a little hidden lake.

One of those perfect days that will stay with you for as long as you live. The type of day that is the reason people fall in love in the spring.

Across the lake we saw him. King of the Canadian north crowned in still velvet glory, majestically plodding into the water and we watched him start to swim across the lake. With a conspiratorial wink and the mischievous glint in his eye that I would come to love so well, Larry angled the canoe towards the moose. As we pulled alongside the agitated forest behemoth, Larry plucked me from my seat and placed me on the moose's back before I even knew what was happening. "Hold tight chum. You are perfectly safe until his feet can touch the lake bottom". Gripping the moose's still velvet antlers, I could feel his muscles rippling and rolling beneath me as I whooped with laughter. A young boy momentarily taming nature's fury, before I knew it and much too quickly Larry pulled me from the moose and back into the canoe. A long moment later the water around the moose began to churn and roil. Giving us one last look before disappearing into the deep woods, I could swear to you Dear Reader that the moose winked at us.

Of course this was to remain our secret, looking back on it now I am sure he was more than a little afraid of my mothers' reaction to our shenanigans.

Larry taught me a different way to view the world and an awful lot about life. It is too his credit when someone calls me "old fashioned" for holding a door or tipping my hat to a lady. I am grateful for these lessons.

Larry lived on his own, in the bush supporting himself from 1916-1991 a real simple man who was easy to look up too, a fair definition of a role model.

Thanksgiving 1991 Larry came to our house for dinner. During dinner Larry said that he was starting to not feel well and didn't look very good. Mom and Dad were able to convince him to go to the hospital rather than head back out to the bush.

Cancer.

For the next couple of days I was able to visit him after school and on the weekends. I got to sit by his side, giving him a steaming cup of tea and listening and learning.

You Dear Reader would not believe the stories, 91 years worth. Some were the comfortable tried and true, some were completely new, going to Detroit to watch Babe Ruth play ball as an example. Knowing on some level that the end was approaching and realizing that I might not get another opportunity, I worked up the courage to ask "the question". Why?

At 14 years old I wanted to know why this loving caring man who had devoted his life to handcrafting toys for children, the man who had held my hand as we walked through my first berry patch full of bears just so I wouldn't be scared. Why spend your life alone? Alone in the bush, no wife, no kids. The look he gave me when I asked that question was both haunted and wistful. "Chum let me tell you about Annabelle."

# 9

"Walking to the river, fishing pole over my shoulder and wearing a new pair of dungarees (I am still not really sure what dungarees are). I shuffled my feet in the sand as I went to catch dinner for my family. My older brother really the fisherman of the family had just left to go give the Hun what for in France so the fishing fell to me. We lost him at Vimy Ridge. My dad had a hard time finding work and despite my brothers' willingness to go and fight for King and Canada we needed to change our last name from Swardfiger to Sward in an attempt to at least quell the anti-German discrimination.

With my head full up of thoughts, I just about missed her sitting there on her porch swing. I stopped dead, right in the middle of the road. An angel surely, I rubbed my eyes and still she sat there, no apparition. Aphrodite made flesh.

Was it with her giggle or the wicked gleam in her eyes? Either way she set her hook and reeled me in with the wave of her hand. Feeling the red rise up from under my collar to colour my cheeks, I hurried on down to the river.

I probably caught our supper. It is hard for me to remember, I was lost in another world, and all my thoughts were consumed by her. Thinking back on it all I wonder why we place so much importance on the mind? Our most important organ is our heart. Have you felt your mind quicken and stir when you hear a beautiful song, or see a pretty face? Have you ever felt anything leap for joy in your head? Does your head ache incessantly at the thought of living without her? Guard your heart chum for it determines the course of your life.

Each day as I walked by her house, I would find her closer and closer to the road. Closer to me...... until one day she was waiting at the end of her lane. As I hurried by with my head held down, she called out to me "BOY!!!" "Hey Boy!" I turned and was almost blinded by her smile "yes emm" was about all I could stammer out. "Boy come here!" she asked me my name and what I was doing each day walking by her house. I answered her as best as my mouth full of mothballs would allow. She must have been satisfied with my answers because with a flick of her hair she ran up her lane.

The next day as I passed her house, my heart dropped to the pit of my stomach when I realized that she wasn't there. It was then I knew in my heart of hearts I needed to see her again.

With a heavy heart I dragged myself onward to my fishing hole. I plopped myself down and watched my bobber lazily float along the river. Under the summer sun I must have just drifted off when a tremendous commotion in the bushes behind me startled me. Out burst my angel. She thumped down next to me and proudly proclaimed "My name is Annabelle by the way."

Soon our summer afternoons were spent side by side, laughing, talking about nothing and getting to know each other. Quickly the distance between us closed, her hand in mine as we sat and then a quick peck on the cheek, a hug when she saw me. Until one day as she was leaving to head home for supper. With what seemed like a racehorse in my chest, I grabbed her arm and pulled her in close. Losing myself for a moment in her eyes, I softly pressed my lips to hers. Her shock quickly passed and she gently settled into the kiss that would change my life. The moment that her lips touched mine I knew that A....Annabelle would hold my heart forever.

Deep inside me I knew in my heart of hearts that Annabelle's parents would never accept a dirt poor German kid from the wrong side of the tracks as a potential match for their daughter. So with a determination that can only be fired and tempered with love I set out to the Lindsay train station."

Maybe I interrupted Larry at this point Dear Reader because my memory from here is a little fuzzy or maybe he succumbed to his pain meds. I have a half remembered story of a clandestine meeting the night before he left, a promise of undying love under the stars and sealed with a kiss.

At the end he started to sing "You're so young and beautiful and I love you soooo. Your lips so red, your eyes that shine, shame the stars that glooow. So fill these lonely arms of mine and kiss me tenderly and you'll be forever young and beautiful to me." Half sung, half mumbled he drifted off to sleep.

The next day the phone rang and though I pedaled my bike faster than I ever had before, when I burst past the nurse and threw myself sobbing into Larry's arms he was already starting to cool. The smile on his face mirrored his last mumbled word "Annabelle".

Larry loved her so much that for 80 years he was never able to love another. I used to think that was so very tragic. All I could see was an old man dying alone. I could only see the waste, not truly understanding his last words to me as he was drifting away "chum, may you be as lucky as to find your Annabelle."

I wish I could tell him now that I understand. To tell him that I know what he meant. Would that I could lead her, arm in mine, so that he could look her over. He would grab her other arm and lead her to the little room off of the workshop, hand her a cup of steaming tea and regal us with tales of years gone by. I can see that secretive conspiratorial wink as he sends me out to the well to fetch some water. When we are ready to leave with his hand on my shoulder, tipping his imaginary hat in her direction, he would whisper in my ear "she be a fine lass chum." Would that I could, I wish I could say "I am glad you met my Annabelle".

In the years that have followed I was able to track down where Annabelle was buried in the Lindsay cemetery. To give you Dear Reader the same closure that I needed, Annabelle died in 1919 at 18 years of age as a result of Spanish flu. Their love however lived and lives on as long as we can tell the tale.

To Larry I never got to say thank you or even to say goodbye. I would like to think that he knew in his heart how I felt and how much his life meant to mine. I know he would have liked her. He would have understood, he would have loved my Annabelle.

# 10

Ok ok….. See I knew it would happen sooner or later. I am actually quite surprised it took so long. The reason you are here is not the day to day survival of the end of the world. You did that. You don't need to rehash those details and why even listen to the stories that brought me here unless there is a reason to be here. I told you, though you no doubt are sceptical that this is a love story. Whether the tale of a love written in the stars or a tale of star crossed lovers you decide? Is it the tale of the kind of love that needs to be shouted from the mountain tops, muted by circumstances? Whatever it is, it is why I sit here today waiting. Most likely inspired by all this talk of Annabelle, last night I dreamt of her.

There is still so much more to tell you, you will need more background for sure, however since she is the reason for this tale let me tell you my dream. A small taste to tide you over until later.

I'm sitting in the living room watching her get ready. I know deep inside, beyond a shadow of a doubt that I am the luckiest man in the world. She is so lovely, beautiful really, that sometimes I feel like I am dreaming my life rather than living it. For surely in the real world I would not deserve a woman such as her.

She takes the dogs leash and a plain black scarf off of the hook by the door, crossing the fringed ends of the scarf over her chest.

Her soft shining hair, a different colour each week, frames her perfectly proportioned face, reminiscent of how I envision Freyja.

Peering through the frost covered glass she shivers and says "36 degrees and only the end of October at this rate we will have snow by Thanksgiving." I laughingly reply "Thanksgiving was 2 weeks ago and jeez 36 degrees I should be digging out my shorts I packed them away too early, and if we get snowed in pretty lady I would gladly spend the winter snowed in with you." Her eyes smoulder as she glares at me.

Those eyes, so clear and expressive, just the perfect colour of hazel. I doubt that anyone could look into those eyes and lie or fail to love the woman beneath.

Grinning she walks over and bends to kiss me. As her lips touch mine that spark, that feeling still rushes to my toes. I gently touch the side of her face and run my hand along her jaw line while whispering "I could spend a lifetime lost in your eyes." She opens her mouth to respond and....

I awaken, cold and alone, the emptiness fills me, loneliness my constant companion. That was our life, that was the dream, what we wanted before it was so cruelly plucked from my heart.

Is she out there? Does she know I love her? I can't give up. I can only hope that she knows that no matter what separates us she is loved completely.

See Dear Reader I told you there would be romance. In fact by the time you are done reading these pages, I am sure you will have had enough mushy love shit to last you a lifetime.

# 11

You could say that Larry's death was the beginning of the end for my childhood. I would still like to talk about my childhood though for a bit before we bid it adieu.

My childhood was a good one, a great one even. So don't jump to any conclusions by the fact that I tried to run away from home. I did that not because not because things were awful at home. I wasn't afraid of my parents per se. Mostly I just hated getting in shit, all of us hate getting in shit, I really hated getting in shit. I was the kind of kid who could look you in the eye and tell you black was red if I felt I was going to avoid getting in shit. A strong desire to try and keep everyone happy all the time, you could label it co-dependant if you need a label.

How I developed like this is really a mystery, it's not like my parents beat me or anything. They did punish me and punishment definitely included spanking but never was it undeserved or excessive. I was whacked lots with flyswatters, broke a few wooden spoons and once mom clocked me pretty good with a wooden rolling pin. Gasp if you must it was only because I taped Willy the kid next door into his sisters Barbie van box and then gave him a ride down the stairs. His anguished screams caused me to rush home and hide under my bed and that's what she could reach me with.

In fact even Willy's dad even paddled me one time, on my sixth birthday. Willy had gotten me one of those suction cup bow and arrow sets and well we were playing with it out in the yard when Willy piped up and bet me next weeks allowance that I could not hit him in the eye. Weelll....I am sure you can surmise where this story is headed. Who knows why we do the things we do as children.

Willy's dad must have seen me shoot poor Willy and he erupted out of his house, chasing me around mine, until.....he finally caught me trying to hide in amongst the sheets hanging on the clothesline. He paddled me pretty good I must say.

This is where we take a break to thank Willy. Later in life archery and bow hunting were a big part of my life and my ability to him a target in the eye with an arrow got me out of some tight scrapes and allowed me to survive up to this point, to even be here to write this tale.

Dad did not have to often resort to spanking. When he did however it was always open handed. Only once did Dad ever actually use his belt. After that the mere threat was enough.

I don't want you to feel cheated Dear Reader because I am not going to go into every little detail of this story. I just want to move on. The gist of it is, when I was in grade 2 in trouble for something I mooned my principal, I trust that you can fill in the blanks. I think it would be safe to say that my parents had a tough go of things.

One thing that I do find mildly amusing is anytime that I mentioned a humorous story that inevitably ended with a flyswatter or a wooden spoon, my mother would make this sanctimonious tongue clicking noise, followed up by her saying something like "well I never", as the idea of spanking your kids has become less popular. It is almost like what ever story I am telling offends her in some way. Well let me tell you, if we could ever find the flyswatter and wooden spoon graveyard and we were able to use the latest techniques for forensic ass print identification, we would find plenty with my latent prints.

I am not bitching I deserved it every time, well at least the times my kid sister wasn't falsely accusing me of something I didn't do. There was no way I could have considered myself hard done by in any sense and didn't. If my parents are guilty of anything it would be loving me too much, and being a bit too indulgent of me following my heart.

# 12

*I* have already mentioned that as a kid I was a voracious reader. I spent hours solving crime with Frank and Joe Hardy, saving the day with "Big Red", relating to the childhood angst in the Judy Blume novels. Before long I was travelling to fantastic realms with Thomas Covenant and discovering evil spacecraft in a backwoods Maine town. Books opened up the world for me.

Just because I was bookish I don't want to leave you with the impression of a small whiny kid, pining away in his bedroom that wishes for a real friend too play with.

In fact as a child I was very gregarious. Our house always seemed to be the centre of neighbourhood activity. There were always people around. Whether street hockey games, hide and seek, tag football, or snowball fights there was always a multitude of children around. Almost every night you could if driving by hear the sounds of children playing out in front of the house or carried on the wind from the back yard.

This was a pattern that would continue for all of my life much to the chagrin of my future ex-wife. Later in life the overheard excited voices were not yelling "Not It!" More likely over cigarettes and beer we could be found arguing over the various fiscal policies of different levels of government, the latest moves by our favourite political parties and a multitude of survival strategies for the impending zombie apocalypse. Not quite like the care free days of childhood where nothing really mattered as long as you were close enough to get your butt home promptly when the streetlights came on.

I know that I have painted a picture of a very care free life. My parents did not neglect adding in responsibilities. Just because I was a kid did not exempt me. I had chores to do around the house for my allowance. We have already talked about snow shovelling and weeding the garden also from the time I was old enough to ride a bike I had a paper route.

Life always has a sense of irony, I used some money from my paper route to but a game for my Nintendo called paperboy the object of the game was to deliver papers. Could you Dear Reader imagine playing a game called office worker, as we got older we left our work at work.

# 13

Too much talk of books and video games could paint a picture for you of kids who spent a lot of time inside. Let me tell you that may have been the ways of parenting in the days just BZE. That may even be what you Dear Reader were used to seeing. As strange as it may seem to you though, as kids we barely watched a half hour of TV a day (only 13 channels and that was cable) we really spent most of our time playing outside.

Our number one playground was on and around Deadman's Lake. Located on the eastern edge of town this small lake and surrounding forest was every kids dream. A plethora of small game for our pellet guns and sling shots, enough northern pike in the water to make taking the canoe out worthwhile (though I wouldn't recommend eating the fish) an ever changing landscape to create childhood adventures. It even provided us with the odd bear, moose, or deer sighting. Crossing over the beaver dam you could find an old mine, as you can see a child's paradise.

My best friend at the time was a kid named Mark Sharp. Sharpie and I were damn near inseparable, kind of like Abbot and Costello or French fries and ketchup; it would have been hard to imagine one without the other.

Deadman's Lake and the surrounding bush was only a few minutes walk from our house's so it really was a natural playground for us. It was where we built our tree forts, shot each other with bb guns before there were paintball guns and where we ran to hide from and escape the big bullies in our neighbourhood.

Charlie.......? Hmmm what was his last name? He once cornered us down by the old stump; he beat us up and then threatened to light our balls on fire if we told on him. LaFortress....That's It! Yep. Charlie LaFortress. Our mothers' uncanny intuition and our dishevelled appearance gave it all away and needless to say we told our moms everything so we spent the next 5 years of our lives in fear for our balls and avoiding Charlie.

The other bully in our neighbourhood was a boy named Ned Skillen. I have no idea or at least can't remember why Ned hated us, but he sure did. He never passed up an opportunity to thump us good. Often on a summer afternoon you could find Mark and I booking it through someone's backyard trying to reach Deadman's Lake and escape from Ned.

Mostly we spent our days in the woods, building jumps for our bikes, tracking small game, building our forts and being bullies ourselves to Mark Brankin our neighbourhood "fairy" our parents forced us to play together and we spent time perfecting the knots we learned in scouts tying up Mark so we could take off on him to play. Trees, rocks and even an ant hill made good tethers for Brankin.

The aforementioned tree fort was the penultimate accomplishment of each year. With each years model more elaborate than the last.

Our first tree fort was a bit of a rite of passage for us. Mark and I chummed around with this other lad named Mike Coagie. Mike's dad had built him a tree fort in his backyard. Partially inspired by jealousy we decided that we would build one for us all by ourselves.

We took the time one afternoon to sit down with some pencil crayons and construction paper and draw up some blue, green and redprints for our first tree fort. Indulge me and allow me to describe this masterpiece to you Dear Reader.

This architectural wonder had multiple levels, with towers, parapets, walls, a rope elevator that worked on a complex series of pulleys, cages for the wild beasts that would help with our defences and a full blown moat which we would dig by hand. Even then I was a dreamer. After drawing up these plans it was time to head out to the garage.

The garage was the treasury where my dad kept all the tools we would need. We gathered up all the hammers, shovels, nails, saws and axes that we felt we would need to build our tree fortress.

We strugglingly loaded all these tools into my yellow wagon and trudged down the driveway. Our plan was to clear cut an area so we could start on the foundation of the building that would protect us from the Neds and Charlies of the world.

We made it about halfway down the driveway when the front door burst open and dad barrelled down on us. Mildly out of breath and surprisingly calmly dad enquired as to why we were headed down the driveway with all of his tools. Mark was quick to point out too one of my dads' withering glares, that we "clearly" didn't have "all" the tools because there was no power outlets down in the bush.

Dad rifled through our wagon full of tools periodically removing one or two with some half muttered words like "hurt yourselves", "cut off your foot", or "Are you crazy!" this last being said for a 15 pound maul that took both Mark and I to lift it into the wagon. After purloining our booty, dad let us continue on our way and we once again set off to build our fortress.

Arriving at the perfect spot, which really meant where we were too tired to pull the wagon anymore. We realized that we had a serious problem. The loss of our "gonna cut your foot off" more commonly known as an axe. We really had no way to chop down the copious amounts of trees we would need to complete our plans.

Being the industrious types that we were, we decided to put our heads together to come up with a solution.

Much like our heroes The 3 Stooges and I would also like to add here this is one of the few times we put our heads together that didn't result in one or both of us making a date with the previously mentioned wooden spoon.

It didn't really take us all that long to hit upon a "brilliant" idea. We would chop down all the trees we would need, with the back end of a claw hammer. Looking back on it now, I have to say we really did have a tremendous amount of determination.

So like two little beavers, armed with our claw hammers we set about the task of cutting down enough trees to build our work of art. We ended up with enough wood to build a small platform between 3 trees and a ladder as well. I can remember the whole project took well over a week.

Upon completion we spent many hours up there, eating our snacks, planning our next great adventure and feeling very safe indeed as we were at least 10 feet up in the trees. I can also remember the pride we felt when our dad's came to inspect our work and they gave it their seal of approval.

If you go even now, down the bike path, turn left at the big rock, follow the trail past the pink lady slippers and stop at the old stump of light your balls on fire fame. Turn due south and take a few paces in look up and you will see one lone branch nailed across 2 trees, and if from there you take the time to look down. You will see the forest floor littered with strangely chewed stumps. Though you may assume the beaver in the lake has dental issues upon closer inspection you will see the marks of the back end of a claw hammer.

Throughout the years that fort was built and rebuilt. I would like to believe that, that one long lasting branch is from the original oh so many years ago.

How quickly did our childhood skill of building a tree fort turn to the life skill of building a permanent tree stand? Many have I built over the years and my times spent sitting still in trees are some of my most treasured memories.

# 14

By the way I want to thank you for staying with me as we wade through some of the more boring but nonetheless defining aspects of childhood. I do however hope that you were able to in your minds eye see the sun dappled forest floor and you were able to smile as you pictured those 2 little boys labouring their hearts out to build their first tree fort.

Since you have come this far Dear Reader, you might as well come along for a while longer yet. I would guess that you might enjoy some of the tales of our youthful hi-jinks. It speaks to a different time when we were safe, when the dead stayed dead. Believe you me us boys were always up too something.

I think I may have left you with the impression of innocent lads traipsing through the bush with our tools or toys flung over our shoulders like little lumberjacks or trappers, with the possible exception of course, when I mentioned tying Mark Brankin to an anthill. Could you blame us really? I mean he played with my little horsey's and caring bears.

To be honest about us boys though, we really did find mischief at just about every turn. The combination of me and Sharpie was like adding gasoline to a fire and inevitably we were getting in trouble. I couldn't even count the number of times I watched Mr. Sharp box Mark's ears while sending me home to get my ears boxed or Mark being in the same but reverse situation.

It wasn't a long walk from Mark's house to mine, all of about 10 minutes. Many a time however passing by the trailer park caused a rising feeling of impending doom because I knew Mrs. Sharp had called ahead.

It really depended on who answered the phone how much trouble I was going to be in. Dad had a fairly easy going demeanour and mostly had a boy's will be boy's attitude. My mother on the other hand could be a different story and if her hackles were raised she could rain down the fury of a gaggle of harpies. How does that old saying go? "Hell hath no fury". I think when William Congreve wrote those famous words he meant to refer too a woman who had been cheated on or perhaps he meant to refer to a woman who had been rejected. Realistically though he never had to deal with my mother after Mark Brankin was rescued or our numerous other poorly planned endeavours, an entire graveyard full of flyswatters and wooden spoons can attest to that fact.

Growing up almost any sentence that started with "Hey let's" or "Do you wanna" usually ended with one or both of us getting "tanned hides". Let me pause here to tell you one thing Dear Reader. Over the years I have had plenty of opportunities to tan a hide or 2 and it bears little to no resemblance to getting a spanking from my mother and requires no flyswatter or wooden spoon. I do also however dare you to tell my mother that. I wish I could.

I also suspect that our youthful hi-jinks would not be measured so harshly in a world rife with crack, pills and teen prostitution. We got our kicks from rearranging our neighbour's lawn ornaments, scattering the clothes off of the clotheslines, lighting off smoke bombs so we could watch the water bombers and garden raiding.

If our offence could not be made right by "tanning our hides", then the next step would inevitably be a "meeting" between our fathers. The outcome of these "meetings" was also preordained. We were often seen being marched by our fathers down to the offended person's house.

With heads held low and downcast eyes we would be forced to apologize and offer some sort of seasonal restitution, mowing lawns, shovelling snow, and raking leaves. I am sure that you get the idea. On a side note I consider this a great parenting technique.

Sometimes I think this meeting of the fathers was as much of a punishment for Dad as it was for me.

# 15

Sitting at my desk and the anticipation is building. I am going to have it out with Fish once the clock strikes 3:30 and the bell rings. Moments after the bell rings a circle of boisterous children forms, the chanting starts.

"FIGHT!", "FIGHT!", "FIGHT!".

After a couple of clumsy punches, it looks much more like a grappling match as us ungainly and awkward pre-teens tumble to the ground rolling around in the mud.

Bursting through the crowd of kids and grabbing us by the scruffs of our necks, Mr. Fish shouted out "What the heck is going on here?"

My friends and I spun a hastily concocted story that involved us playing a game and used words like "horsing around". For a moment it looked like Mr. Fish wasn't going to buy what we were selling and then he said "oh, ok then let's go Sean." I swear we had just got off scot-free when that little weenie looked at his father and said "no dad we were fighting."

Seriously, who does that? I mean come on......scot-free. Needless to say my dad had to field a phone call that night. A "meeting" was set for six the next morning at the local coffee shop.

We arrived promptly and Mr. Fish immediately jumped up on his soapbox, he rallied against my "un-provoked" aggression. Dad could hardly get a word in edgewise.

The gleam in Sean's eyes and the cat that caught the canary smile made me want to "wipe" that smirk off of his face. I was however able to restrain my desires.

Eventually after much haranguing and brow beating on Mr. Fish's part, we reached some semblance of a compromise. I was forced to apologize and hand shakes were exchanged all around.

As we were leaving I am pretty sure I heard my dad mutter something under his breath like "I wish I could have had the opportunity to meet him in the schoolyard." This left me believing that dad felt Mr. Fish was as much of a weenie as I knew Sean was.

You know what Dear Reader, as I go through this process I stumble across some memories that make me smile, even all these years later. It is these moments of happiness that make it so imperative that mankind survive. I think that though I was grounded that day it wasn't because I beat Sean up. I believe that I was grounded because Dad had to get up at six in the morning to go have coffee with Weenie and Weenie Jr. I can't help but smile when I remember the man that my father was.

# 16

*I* can't always predict where this story will take me Dear Reader. I definitely have not given you enough background to jump right into the tale that I really want to tell. I close my eyes and I see her next to me. I fall asleep and she haunts my dreams. Love is the greatest, worst feeling in the world. I wonder if love is strong enough to survive life.

I just again want to take a moment to tell you that I appreciate your continued patience with my story Dear Reader. It does help with the loneliness.

The truth about life, any life, is that it is only a collected series of days. Simple enough concept eh. The thing that is so wonderful about life is its unpredictability.

Pressure is brought to bear on us and our lives are forever altered by events that we couldn't possibly have foreseen.

We leave our houses every morning, to take the dog for a walk, go to work, or maybe even to do some shopping. Ninety nine times out of a hundred we return home without a single thing happening to us that we will remember even a month in the future. On these days our life is swept away with the daily boredom of living. We are caught up in the basic hum drum of everyday existence. Plodding along one foot in front of the other, trudging glumly to our grave.

It is that other day, the "magic" day for which we truly live. Eventually this will be a story of that "magic", with only the banality of living everyday life mixed up in between. If one can refer to the dead rising up to claim civilization as banal.

Is this yet again one of my cliff hangers, put here to tease, and designed to keep you coming back for more.

The "Magic" day, well we will see.

It is on these "magic" days that our character becomes defined, our spiritual growth is accelerated and our emotional shifts are made. Sometimes, maybe once in a lifetime, there will be a whole string of these days one after the other. Days so full of life and change and challenge that we are completely transformed by the experience and our hearts become overfilled with limitless love. We can be overwhelmed by the simple miracle of being alive.

This will when all said and done be a story of such a time, I promise you Dear Reader. A story that could define true love. To truly grasp the scope I am trying for, I believe I must give you a bit more background, for I believe that to understand our future we must comprehend our past. Our past is the cornerstone on which our futures foundations are built.

# 17

*I* think that is enough waxing philosophical for a bit, enough of me teasing you with what's to come. I believe I had just finished telling you a story about Sean Fish. That particular fist fight was just one of many that we had over the years. Sean was in just about every one of my classes from kindergarten straight through to grade 13. For whatever reason we seemed to come to blows at least once a year, he was for me the definition of a nemesis. If I was the hero, he was the villain or vice versa. His only goal in life seemed to be to place ahead of me, whether in athletics or academics. Most of the time we jostled each other for position and managed to maintain an uneasy truce, he was my North Korea.

I can only hope that when all the craziness began that he was disembowelled quickly. I don't wish that he suffered; I would like to think that I have outgrown our childish competitions. That being said I do get some perverse pleasure from knowing that I survived and most likely he didn't. Ha ha ha, in your face Fish. Ok ok......I will admit to a little childishness hanging on.

Our boyish competition turned fierce the first year of high school. The main reason for this was a completely hitherto unknown factor, the "girl".

Previous to high school our experience with this strange creature consisted of some hair pulling, it was something we chased through the school yard while pulling on the tendons of partridge feet so they would appear to be grasping for them and something to be pushed into a snow bank at every opportunity. The most dreaded sub-species being the big or little sister. I was slightly ahead of the curve because I could draw on my previous bible camp experiences.

All of that experience was however about to be thrown out of the window and our live were to be irrevocably changed. The catalyst for this change we will call Tanya. Period 4, day one, English class. White sweater, blue jeans, her hair done up just right. When she walked into a room you could not help but take a second look. She had the kind of smile that only those special eclipse viewing glasses could protect you from. It lit up the entire room and was just as contagious and equally fatal to a heart as the dread viruses Ebola Zaire or Marburg.

The desk she chose was next to mine and I was immediately awestruck. My teenage brain backed up and gridlocked at her smile. Unable to perform anything as complex as communication, I was lost in my mind, spinning my wheels while searching for the ever elusive "Hi".

On Tanya's other side....yep you guessed it, Fish. Much to my chagrin he instantly struck up a conversation and within minutes he had her beaming and laughing. Some deep seeded and primordial instinct kicked in and on auto pilot I was able to capture her attention.

By the end of class we had exchanged phone numbers, much again to my chagrin, she also gave her number to Fish. The spirit of competition alive and well in me I decided to make her mine. My motives may not have been as pure as snow however what started as a challenge ended in love.

Tanya lived about 30 kilometres away from my house so a lot of our time together was spent on the phone until we were old enough to drive. Early on I am sure Mrs. Delong our English teacher noticed the similarities in our homework answers for "A Cue for Treason" and "The Merchant of Venice". When she could come into town I would head down to her mom's place and we would walk over to the A&W for a root beer shake, then we would walk around hand in hand.

I know I am making it all sound so pure and innocent. In some ways it really was, at the same time I am talking about a girl who once presented me with a list entitled "50 ways I want to fuck before I die". This list included such standards as "in front of a fireplace on a cold winters night" or "as dessert after a romantic dinner", to the outrageous "as a class presentation".

The great secret to our success was the fact that we were best friends, and we respected each other.

Despite her list we waited a long time and we gave our virginity to each other the summer I turned 19. I may have been 18 but it was the summer I turned 19, so give or take a day or two.

# 18

*I* can totally understand your consternation at this point Dear Reader, with both this tale and my style of narrative. I mean.....come on in all but a few lines we have gone from 14 years of age to 19 years old. At points I am clearly going to have to back track. The tale I have to tell would defiantly be incomplete with all the teenage years and angst removed. So let us go back to grade 9.

When Tanya gave me her phone number thank god that it was period 4. All I could think of was giving her a call. I wish I had the proper words to describe to you Dear Reader how I felt on my way home and all through supper. Nervous, anxious, scared would be a few inadequate words. Pacing up and down the hallway after supper until finally getting up the nerve to pick up the phone.

A bead of sweat forming on my forehead and my fingers were shaking as I started to dial....936-1057....can you believe that Dear Reader I remember the number still over 21 years since that first night, that first phone call. It was with a wavering voice (let's be honest it is hard to talk when your heart is jammed in your throat) that I asked her father if Tanya "was there?"

She came to the phone and my very debonair "hello" must have impressed her because it was 5 years before we hung up the phone. It must have caused a lot of problems for the people at both of our houses who needed to use the phone as well as irritated the hundreds of people who had their "beeps" ignored.

I also do not want to leave you with the impression that I spent my teenage years on the phone.

Briefly we have talked about a first kiss. A snuck out in the middle of the night first kiss behind cabin 4, two lips quickly touch and then we rushed into our respective cabin before we would have to exchange any "words". Since I have set that precedent I will tell you Dear Reader about a few other first kisses as they come up in this tale. Before we go too much further though, let us go back for a bit, back to Deadmans Lake.

# 19

*I* dreamt of her again, I know I promised to take you down to Deadmans Lake with me; however before we do that though let me tell you my dream while it is still fresh in my head.

The house is always the same, open concept living room with a huge picture window that overlooks the lake. Right now it is dark and framed against the window I can only see her silhouette.

With the tiniest hitch of her shoulders I can tell that she has been crying and it breaks my heart.

I walk to her slowly and stand behind her not knowing what to say, not wanting to take her moment away by wrapping my arms around her.

Turning to me she puts her hand on my arm. It is a signal, a gesture to tell me that it is ok for me to touch her back, to pull her close and just hold her.

I did.

I could feel the familiar yet always unique sensation of her soft body just closing in and moulding itself to mine. I held her tightly, feeling her return the embrace with a need that transcended anything physical or sexual.

I could feel the barriers coming down and I knew that she was letting me in. Into a place that had been hollow and cold for a long time like a forgotten cellar.

We stood like that, by the window, just holding each other. I have no idea for how long we stood. Saying nothing, not moving just savouring the closeness of another person, not wrapped up in some phony romance/lust thing.

This was different. Different than anything I had ever experienced. I could not doubt my feelings. I knew they were based on the most primal of emotions. She leaned into me. Her hands moved to the back of my neck, to the sides of my face.

She gently directed the angle of my jaw and she kissed me so damn softly. Her lips so full, so soft and gentle, I can't remember enjoying the simple union of a kiss so totally. The moment hung suspended like a raindrop trapped in a gossamer spider's web. Fragile and beautiful.

Passions door gently creaking open with our first touch, now burst its hinges. Like a wind from the east desire hurricaned in. I took her hand in mine and drew it down across my chest, while turning it to cup her breast. Her back arched from the touch and I could feel the energy spark between us. We wanted each other and it was a good clean honest wanting. We needed it. Slowly, sliding my hand to the flare of her hip, I .........woke up.

It is enough to drive a man mad this longing, to have seen and tasted love. I will wait, fate will decide.

While we wait let us go down and play at Deadmans Lake.

# 20

So far we have had some fun down here eh! I am sure Dear Reader that in the context of a childhood playgrounds you can picture those little boys building tree forts or running around with our pellet guns, time for a tangent I suppose.

I should have realized at a young age that my future would have zombies in it.

On this particular summer day, you know the kind; the sun is too hot even in the shade. There is no hint of a cooling breeze. The entire world seems to be stilled. A day designed for lazing around or for mischievous boys to get up to something.

I would like you to try and imagine the scene as I set it up for you. Two little boys, armed with our pellet guns, a single blade of grass hanging from each of our mouths, creeping slowly and soundlessly through the forest in search of enough squirrels to have for supper tonight. As a young boy nothing seems to bring as much pleasure as bringing home supper, whether fresh walleye just caught up at Flat Rock or enough squirrels to feed the family. The only thing that I can think of that compares to that childlike joy would be bringing that first dandelion bouquet in the house for your mother just because you love her.

Anyway let us rejoin our two brave hunters; we had two squirrels each hanging from our belt loops. Quietly creeping, not even talking, we are listening intently for the tell tale rustling of a squirrel in the fallen leaves and pine needles on the forest floor or the angry chattering that will warn the other squirrels of our dangerous presence or even a falling pine cone thrown from Mr. Squirrels perceived position of safety on a branch above our heads.

A slow rustling halts our creeping and holds our attention. Mark's hand shoots out and quickly grabs a small snapping turtle off the forest floor. Did you know that a snapping turtle has seven different textures of meat? I am partial to five of them. Dad had shown me a fast way to clean them with a hacksaw and a chisel. I suggested Mark should shoot him in the head and then we could have turtle and squirrel stew for supper.

Mark set the turtle down so he could get a clear shot, just a little too close, and the turtle snapped out and grabbed a hold of Sharpie's leg. The high pitched keening and the ensuing chaos led us to an unprecedented expenditure of fire power. To my young mind it must have rivalled the gun fight at the OK Corral. Instead of Wild West bad guys our arsenal was unloaded onto or more accurately into our hapless snapping turtle.

Head completely severed (we had to use needle nose pliers to remove it from Sharpie's leg), the turtle could have been used for a baby rattle when we picked him up because of the amount of BB's and pellets in him. Much to our surprise that turtle started to walk away.

A small boy's lack of understanding of the concept of a chicken running with its head cut off and with an inability to comprehend the complex firings of the central nervous system, lead not surprisingly to stories of turtle possession and our very first encounter with the walking dead.

Being tough little boys we both walked away from that turtle. Neither one of us wanted to give in to the dread seeping in by running and thus be forever branded a "chicken".

I wish our undead; the undead of the here and now were so simple to walk away from. We were lucky; we didn't have to face the fast running zombie as envisioned in the 28 days trilogy. Instead the real undead were husks of their former humanity, lumbering forward in their never ending search for the flesh of the living. Once the shock and terror wear off, usually after your first couple of encounters, I believe that it is natural for the human mind to start to want answers by forming questions like

"What happens to the zombies after having consumed so much flesh?" It stands to reason that once you were dead all digestion would cease, right? So would the zombie not eventually be so weighted down carrying all that dead flesh in their stomachs they just wouldn't be able to lurch and lumber in search of more? A person when full to bursting will search out the nearest couch and go lay down while holding his belly. We have all seen the men in our families do this after thanksgiving dinner. I have yet to come across a zombie all laid out in a ditch, holding his belly, who cries out "I'll get to you in a minute, I just have to let this settle!" or "Hold on I just gotta take the browns to the super bowl. Then I will be as right as rain."

I know, I know but I warned you about my sense of humour. I remember another off colour joke about developing a picture and I can't help but think of her she was there when I first heard it.......

Standing almost out of sight on the deck, she stands on the end of the dock as the sun goes down. Her long hair blows softly in the breeze and she is perfectly framed by the last pink rays of the sun. It is almost like she is on display, a perfectly designed advertisement that wants to sell me happiness, in a bottle, or a spray, something that I can consume. I am sold.

I am overcome by my big baritone wracking sobs. I am by myself here, without her I now know what it feels like to be alone, only because with her by my side I was able to feel what it was like to be whole.

Alas again my tangents cause me to jump the gun. I was in the process of talking about first kisses and off we go chasing little boys and squirrels and a zombie turtle. I just about gave it all away by telling you about my last first kiss. So let's go back, let us talk a little more about Tanya.

# 21

November has replaced September as the point in time where our narrative takes place. Tanya and I were at a friend's house for his birthday. A peripheral player in this tale at best but a good friend at the time nonetheless, we will call him Denis.

If you would indulge me here once more for a side note worth mentioning here is, one of the drunkest I have ever been in my life was with Denis, his dad and some other friends on a moose hunting trip. I must have been about 17 or so. Sitting around the campfire, Denis and I decided in our youthful exuberance that we were going to out drink Denis's father. Now if you have ever had the "pleasure" of watching me drink beer you will know that this story did not have a pretty ending. Though my memory is very hazy for obvious reasons at some point in the night Denis's father stopped my wavering self from collapsing into the fire.

My next clear memory is waking up the next morning to Denis's fathers incessant whistling and the nauseating smell of bacon frying. Through gummed up half open eyes I saw a chipmunk inches from my face, happily munching away in a puddle of my puke. Like a black bolt of lightning Beaner, Denis's dog chomped that chipmunk right out of the puke.

It seems so strange to me how the mind works Dear Reader. One minute I am about to tell you about my first kiss of any substance and instead we veer off and you end up reading about a puke eating chipmunk getting torn in half by a small terrier named Beaner. I guess you don't now have any trouble with my attention deficit diagnosis.

I may just be avoiding talking about that kiss because inevitably any talk of kissing will eventually lead to "the kiss". Anyways enough of my armchair psychology.

I may not be ready to go there just yet but let me say, we aren't all blessed to have that kiss in our lifetimes. Those of us who are welll....it's a single kiss that will change the direction of your life....such a kiss.

I miss her you know. Even now as I write this I can almost hear her voice. I can faintly hear her approaching and bits and pieces of her laughter on the wind. I get dazzled by her smile when I close my eyes and I ache all over without her in my arms.

We have all lost so much Dear Reader. In telling this tale I keep her close to my heart. My heart is all I have left. I am trying to not be melancholic, let us get back to Tanya.

# 22

anya was impatient if I remember correctly. Looking back with the benefit of hindsight I can't say as I blame her. The boys outnumbered the girls at this party by at least 3 to 1. I am sure she was tired of video games and talking about the useless things 14/15 year old boys talk about like hockey, video games, girls, hockey, girls, music and girls.

Tanya had a "tone". This is not unique to Tanya in fact from my mother on down every girl I have ever met has not just one but a variety tones. Each girl's tones are individual and unique yet it seems that their meanings are universal. So my experience teaches me each girl has a series of tones that they use in conversation to convey various meanings. The one thing that you can however take to the bank is, if a girl is using a tone with you, you had better get the meaning right or come hell or high water you are going to be miserable for the next little while. It has also been my experience that a little while can be a very long time.

I learned in first year psychology that 90 percent of all human is nonverbal. I believe a full 40 percent of female communication is done through tones.

This particular tone of Tanya's not only implied that she was unimpressed but also that she was bored. The use of this tone made it clear to me that she felt it was my responsibility to alleviate her boredom. She suggested that we leave the party and go for a walk while using her tone.

Taking only a moment to congratulate myself on my ability to both recognize and decipher the "tone", as I quickly realized I would have to be at my best because there is nothing more dangerous or unpredictable (remember I hunt bears) than going for a "walk" with a bored and unimpressed teenage girl who has "expectations" that you will be able to change this for her somehow.

I wouldn't hesitate to say that my debonair nature, acerbic wit and irresistible charm won the night, rather than admit I was probably just the best of a long list of bad choices. So I am going to completely disregard the latter. After all it is my story and I should be able to tell it how I want too. We are all guilty of a little revisionist history.

Sooo...due to my utter irresistibility we ended up in this year's incarnation of the "tree fort" on the far side of Deadmans Lake. We climbed up the rope ladder and sat huddled together under the moon and we talked. This talking was easy to do as it was very similar to the talking we had been doing for a couple of months now on the phone.

All of a sudden or at least to me it seemed sudden Tanya looked at me with odd look. This was a look I had never before encountered, and she said "Look Greg are you ever going to kiss me or what?" She then proceeded to list off every blown opportunity I had had to kiss her. As she prattled on and on, and mostly to shut her up, I quickly leaned in and kissed her, she definitely shut up and as soon as she recovered from her initial shock she kissed me back.

After an eternal second we broke our kiss and while staring into her deep brown eyes, she half whispered "What took you so long?" I couldn't help it I burst out laughing. I'm not going to lie, I was a little afraid she was going to be mad. I mean women are so unpredictable until she burst out laughing too.

We spent the rest of the evening there talking, laughing and kissing.

When the time came (well before midnight to avoid the lost souls. Seriously.)I walked her to her mom's house and we sang "Fishin in the Dark" hand in hand. This is the first time I can remember connecting a song to an event. Being so close on the heels of Larry's death this was a time in my life when I was learning some real life lessons. I learned about death, grief, joy, and love all at the same time. Every time I hear "You and me going fishin' in the dark" I can't help but almost hear her laugh, taste her lips and yearn for the innocence that we once had.

I can remember floating home my feet six inches off of the sidewalk. Little did I know then that I was learning the skills I would need one day to love her.

Just so you know I am not being deliberately obtuse when I speak of her, because when all said and done this tale will be a tale of her. Everything in its place. When it comes time to put me in the ground (please, making sure my brain stem is severed) I would like it to be said that I loved her truly and that we had a once in a lifetime love, maybe play that old George Jones song "He stopped loving her today". Really as I keep begging you Dear Reader just bear with me for a moment more and we will get there. Go back to the beginning if you must but I warned you I really did.

# 23

Looking back now Larry's death was probably the first brick in the wall of life that I carried on my shoulders. Each successive brick weighed me down a little more. These years were good years the last I had for a long, long time besides Tanya and my friends I had football and skiing.

Around the time I was 8 or 9 years old my dad asked me to choose between skiing and hockey for the winter sport I was to participate in. It was too much for him to drive me to hockey practice and out to the ski hill, so I needed to pick one or the other, and I chose skiing.

I loved the freedom, the way it felt as you raced down the hill. The sensation of your edges carving smoothly through the snow, your tight muscles guiding you through the powder, free, no thoughts, just being, really being alive.

Or was it the feel of your cleats digging into the grass, every muscle poised on a precipice, on a hair trigger, your heart beginning to pound as you visualized your line. The snap, the rush, BAM!!! It was all so thrilling I loved being alive.

Then one day, one play, one hit, CRACK!!! Hit in the shoulders from the front and the waist from behind. I can remember lying in the grass, staring up at a beautiful blue sky. Trying, willing myself to get up and being confused, not understanding why I wasn't up. It didn't hurt; there was no pain, such confusion, chaos really. People crowded all around a blur of sounds. "Are you ok?", "Can you feel this?" A static hiss of faces, coaches, refs, players, "My God!", "His back!", "His neck!", "Don't touch him!". A veritable cacophony of confusion, unable to move surrounded by cloughing chaos, just wanting to get up and play, trying to be brave "I'll be back by the fourth", "We got this guys", "fucking dirty hit", not knowing not understanding what that snap meant, brick two.

Before proceeding to much further I want to talk with you Dear Reader for a little bit about this whole process and since you have decided to stay thus far, let's have the conversation, about what this writing means to me.

Alone at night has it been days or has it been weeks since I have seen another living human being? The isolation is a terrible shroud to wear. Sitting here by the fire thinking about a life that has been lost and the price of love. Can you Dear Reader imagine what it is like to be motivated to accomplish today by the memory of a smile? To ache for a life hidden within the promise of those eyes? The pain is so intense; this putting pen to paper provides the relief of a bloodletting. Those teenagers who cut themselves would understand what I am talking about. The razor separates the skin in the same way my pencil separates my life. As long as I am writing I am letting out my pain.

Ok .....back to it. I can remember how much I hated the doctor when he walked into my hospital room holding those x-rays. L-4 and L-5 were broken and the vertebrate had slid forward pinching some of my nerves going down into my legs. "Forty percent chance", "surgery", "wheel chair", "brace" all words that swam through the cloud of hatred, managing to penetrate, to sink in. "FUCK YOU!!!!!!!!!" I can remember screaming at him "FUCK YOU I will be skiing by December!!!". Moments of lucidity, waves of pain, waves of drug induced euphoria, days passed this way slowly turning into weeks. Learning to roll myself out of bed, a torture device I had to put on with huge steel braces, much like a corset in the front. Becoming just an inferno of will fuelled only by anger, I pushed myself on and I grew.

The doctors were waiting for my next growth spurt before they would perform any surgery and eventually the day came. I was off to Thunder Bay.

I lay in that hospital bed for 3 months. I had nurses coming in to flip me like a steak on a barbeque. I was a Petri dish of medications and I had reactions that varied from hives to hallucinations. I called out in the night for my dad as my curtains became snakes and spiders that attacked me.

Roommates came and went. One night in the bed next to me Luc just died. He was my friend. We spent the long hours in each other company just talking. We were talking and he just started dying, not the peaceful drawing of his last breath while he gently closed his eyes like Hollywood would portray. What could only be described as death throes occurred and I was unable to even turn myself away as I watched my companion die.

The nurses whirled around and responded to the various alarms and machines with a choreographed chaos. Luc was only 15 and he slipped away right in front of me. I learned that day how helpless we really are when the grim reaper comes to collect his due.

I wonder, as the world collapsed and the dead arose to claim the ashes of civilization, did Luc's reanimated corpse, really little more than skeletal remains, did he walk? Did he have any friends left who even remembered him over 20 years later? Did his mother long for him to come home, just so she could tell him that she loved him before he tore her apart and she joined him in the state of undeath?

If it happened that way I would like to believe, I would hope anyway that there was enough of a spark left. In those last seconds before he ripped out his own mother's throat, that Luc knew and his mother knew he knew that he was loved. That idea holds for me it's own kind of beauty hidden in the horror.

# 24

*I* know the last words I spoke to her were "I love you". So even as I wait I can have some peace in the idea that she knew that she was loved. It must be from all this talk of football, let me share with you last night's dream.

Even through the glass of the window I could feel a surge of excitement ripple through the crowd. Everyone was yelling, chanting a name in unison. Then it hit me like a Mack truck barrelling down on a moose frozen in a hairpin turn.

That's my son they are yelling for!

On the first play from scrimmage, my boy, faked a hand off into the line, and rolled right on a naked bootleg. The fake was so perfect the linebackers were all jammed up in the middle trying to stop the bruising fullback, while my boy stood off in the flat, hands at his sides as though calmly watching the play unfold.

Even the crowd didn't realize that my boy still had the ball, resting it casually against his thigh.

Stepping up, suddenly bringing the ball up, my boy launched a perfect spiral on a perfect arc, forty yards downfield. The entire stadium seemed to catch it's breath as it watched the ball drop into the receivers outstretched hands as he ran down the sidelines on full afterburners.

It was a highlight reel play, complete with the receiver pulling away from the only man who might have tackled him and he showboated and high stepped his way into the end zone. It was a stunning and balls out way to open up a football game.

The eruption from the crowd shook the foundation of the stadium, rattling the glass of the VIP box. People in the stands went instantly crazy. "YEEEEAAHHH!!!!" I screamed "That's my son!!! That's my boy!!!!"

Out of the corner of my eye I caught her giving me a bemused "boys will be boys" look. I was immediately struck by her beauty. Though the years had passed the tiny crows feet served to frame her beautiful eyes rather than age them. The love I felt for her threatened to burst my heart so I gathered her up in my arms. Holding her close while dancing and jumping around "That's our son!!!! That's our boy!!!!" I woke with a smile at least.

This bloodletting only temporarily dulls the pain of wanting to tell her that I love her. The ache of wanting to hold her again.

One day at a time, maybe I need one of those 12 step meetings. You probably remember them, they had little sayings they called slogans like "one day at a time", or "there but for the grace of god go I". The all-time favourite being the serenity prayer "God grant me the serenity to accept the things I cannot change. The courage to change the things I can and the wisdom to know the difference." Could such a simple prayer save me, in a world where Gehenna has cast up her captured souls and tasked them with swelling her ranks?

Would god listen to my feeble cries? Probably. I may be the only one left to cry up to heaven. Mankind has crumbled; the civilization we built has turned to ash. Our hubris will be erased in all but a few short centuries. What monument could have man erected to preserve itself? None I say. There isn't one that could outshine man's legacy if I have anything to say about it.

Should mankind pick itself up and dust itself off after crawling out from whatever cave or crevasse we have hidden in. should someone stumble upon these pages and should they then be able to decipher my chicken scratch. Then my tale, the story of me, though normal at times, plain in others and shear boredom hinted at within these pages, well let this tale be a testament to mankind's greatest characteristic our innate ability to love one another despite tremendous adversity.

Wouldn't that be something, my words survive as a celebration of humanity's ability to love. A million words have been written about the inherent evil nature of man.

Golding paints us a gruesome picture of how quickly man will revert to savagery. Shakespeare knew that greed, lust and power could drive us and Macbeth. The writers of the Greek tragedies' knew we could not escape our fate just ask Oedipus Rex.

It seems that mankind has always understood the darkness within itself. Remove societies constraints, take away the mould of civilization and man will revert to the beast inside. Turning on one another for even the slightest of perceived injustices, in extreme cases of desperation man will even consume man to survive given no other alternatives. Just ask a certain South American soccer team and plan to bring your own food if someone invites you to a Donner party.

# 25

Early on in this narrative, right around page 3, I believe, I told you that I really had no idea why the dead awoke, as to why corpses rose up to consume the living and tear down all that man had built up.

I suppose we know each other well enough now Dear Reader that I can at least share with you my personal pet theory. The Romero's and the Brook's of the world were wrong. We didn't need to look outside of ourselves for the cause. The evil inside of us all was the cause. It waited; it grew, until finally it was strong enough. Man's inherent evil, grew on hatred, powered by holocausts, the screams of the tormented billowed its sails, tears of the persecuted filled its tanks, until finally it had the power to animate its own.

So the dead came back. I can anticipate your next question Dear Reader. With all of this evil why am I able to sit here writing this tale? I believe I survived because I have a reason and because I have been blessed with an abundance of love. At times it would have been easy to give up. To lie down and die, I said I would meet her here so here I have to be.

I guess it is time to get back to my tale, not just the random thoughts running through my head.

Since you are still with me I can only assume Dear Reader that you want me to continue. Though I have said often enough that I wouldn't blame you if you set down these pages and walked away, yet you are still here so I guess you want to hear the rest and I have nothing better to do than oblige you so...... where were we?

Where did we leave off, give me a second to flip back... oh yes. I left the tale with Luc finally losing his battle with cancer. I was left alone in a hospital room with the drug induced snakes and other creepy crawlies, and the memory of watching my friend die.

It is strange looking back on that time now. It could have or maybe should have affected me differently but then again hospitals are the place you go to too hear bad news, "you may not walk again", "lost a long battle". People in the hospital eventually lose so I guess I wasn't all that surprised when Luc finally lost his battle.

A few weeks later the doctors finally let me go home. It wasn't a triumphant homecoming. I was quietly helped into the house and I was laid in my own bed. Much like a newborn baby it was a major accomplishment for me to be able to roll myself over. In some ways as I read this

I hate that I sound so cold, minimizing a death, while cheering my ability to roll over. After all I have seen and after all I have done is it any wonder that I have become desensitized. Hard heartedly I can talk straight deadpan about Luc "losing his battle", let us be honest that is never pretty, I am sure though it was appropriately traumatic at the time.

One of the things that still bother's me to this day about the time when I couldn't roll myself over is missing Joe Carter hit his famous 1993 World Series winning home run. That's right, judge away, a baseball game. At the time I was a huge baseball fan. It was still almost a year away from the great disillusionment, when the fat cat players and the equally greedy owners would selfishly cancel the World Series due to their inability to come to an agreement. 1993 was the second year in a row that the team I grew up idolizing won the World Series.

Just think for a teenage boy, this was the stuff of movie magic brought to life. Hitting a homerun to win the World Series, truly truly amazing, it was something you saw in a hundred baseball movies. It was the ultimate fantasy of every kid who had ever picked up a stick and a ball, in any vacant lot or empty schoolyard. "And the crowd goes wild!" cupping his hands to simulate the roar of the fans, seeing in his minds eye, the ball rise and as it gently slopes down just squeaking over the fence making him the great baseball hero carried on shoulders around the field.

See it happened, it really happened, little sandlot Joe Carter's dream came true. He smashed a homerun to win the World Series ......15 minutes after the nurse turned me away from the TV.

Is this turning away a metaphor is that why I am remembering it now? A metaphor for a dream not witnessed, for a dream that cannot be. Does it mean that true love is the ultimate form of arrogance and God in his infinite wisdom has rolled me over at the triumphal moment, just as we were about to breath life into our love? Such philosophical rambling is the curse of a mind left alone.

# 26

It amazes me how vivid my dreams can be.

I turn and look at her, gazing deep into her captivating eyes. She pushes herself against me with a shyness I have not felt in many years. Her first kiss on my neck more intoxicating than the haze of smoke that surrounds me, and I realize I have been deceiving myself. I didn't smoke to soothe my nerves, to relax, to guarantee a good nights sleep. I needed it to give me the courage to seduce her.....or to be seduced. Could she sense the depth of my loneliness? Could she have known of my disenchantment with life?

She moves her hands over me with an increasing excitement and I am amazed at what the sense of touch can convey. How could she give rise to such exquisite longing? A ridiculously romantic notion pops into my head, what would it be like to make love with her? A fantasy of unmatched passion, of sweet tenderness and pure hot sex in perfect balance. Every muscle flexing and contracting in perfect harmony or at times in breathless counterpoint. Each stroke crying out in mutual surrender, two becoming one. The outer world of reason, my logical mind overwhelmed by the inner world of my feelings and emotion. No wrong words, no sigh mistimed, our bodies moving and meshing in exactly the same mysterious rhythms' by which the great tidal forces of the universe ebb and flow. Raising the act above mere biology, making it a mystical experience......I settle for holding her close, her body nestled into mine and we can feel the love being born between us.

Just a dream and a beginning, a chance to taste, getting close, almost to touch our love.

I awaken. I am alone in a barren room, lying on a worn and creaky mattress, a bare bulb weaves too and fro causing the shadows in the corners to dance and flit like so many demons waiting to claim my soul.

I hear their mocking laughter "FOOL!", "MADNESS!", "FOOL TO BELIEVE, LOVE HAS DIED!". The weight of their words is crushing me.

I truly awaken and I am alone. I wonder what these dreams can foretell, what is my future. Is it to be alone and struggling with encompassing loneliness or was I right true love does exist; love endures and will conquer all. Humanities last footprint on the earth, not made of carbon, but made of love. I suppose I should just return to my tale Dear Reader.

# 27

*I* find it funny where the mind can take you. As I sat down with my pencil I fully intended to talk a little bit about drugs. The sneaking and insidious way they can worm their way into your life and wreak havoc upon it. You know the story don't you?

If one makes you feel better, or makes you feel like you fit in or are ten feet tall and bullet proof. Then two should be even better, and then comes four etc, etc.

I wanted to write about that but see I started thinking about footprints, and the whole crazy idea of a carbon footprint. Carbon footprint was a term that was used BZE to describe a human being's impact on the environment. The definition being "a measure of the total amount of carbon dioxide and methane emissions of a defined population, system or activity, considering all relevant sources, sinks and storage within the spatial and temporal boundary of the population, system or activity of interest. Calculated as carbon dioxide equivalent using the relevant 100 year global warming potential." High falooting malarkey. This term was coined back when people bought into global warming hook, line and sinker.

People switched from cars to bicycles and washed their clothes at midnight in cold water to save energy. Whole governments leap frogged each other to poverty by paying exorbitant amounts for "green" technology. All in an effort to reduce a "carbon footprint". The zombies fixed that little problem thank you very much.

It would almost be laughable if so many hadn't been fleeced. In the time BZE environmentalism was almost as fanatical as radical Islam and the punishment for being an infidel, or an anti, though not crucifixion could include being ridiculed and ostracized as a pariah. Well I survived so eat your hearts out all you granola crunching, tree hugging hippies.

As I think about cause and effect it was inevitable that my thought would drift to me starting to think about my legacy. It may seem strange to you for a guy alone to be thinking about what he will leave behind. I don't even know if anyone else survived? Why else write all this down if not in hopes of a legacy.

I feel I invested a lot of myself into trying to make the world a better place for others. I would also like to believe that I succeeded in my own way more than I failed. Fortunately or unfortunately no matter how much I have accomplished I will only be remembered for this one last love. It is kind of a shame that a whole life can be defined by one act. Mind you if you have to be remembered for only one thing, it is better it be for love I think. Since you are still here Dear Reader I will assume that A) you have too much time on your hands B) this is the last book left or C) you are enjoying the tale.

Ok come on, admit it, I won't tell, humour me. You like this glimpse into my soul, I know you do. You are from a generation that venerated those who were willing to bare their souls. It was just called "reality" TV. Let us call this reality storytelling. If I was allowed one hope it would be that you get a bit of a glimpse into your own soul while you are at it.

I know that I have mentioned drugs a time or two and they may yet find their place in this tale, however, drugs despite Nancy Reagan's promise while not doing me any favours have yet to turn my brain into breakfast. I must go where my muse takes me and right now all I can see is the kitchen at Deer Trail Lodge.

I am not sure why the kitchen? It was a pretty normal kitchen in every respect and nothing really stands out about it. It is however where my time at Deer Trail began. I can remember asking my dad to get something for me and him replying "I'll do you one better and get you a job." I think he even drove me out there for the interview.

The main lodge was huge, made of logs and every-thing you would expect to find at a hunting and fishing camp. Built in 1933 out of rough hewn logs, the walls were adorned with various animal heads and mounted fish. The 33 pound lake trout that hangs above the door to the kitchen and the 460 pound black bear rug that is behind the bar are two of my later additions.

Being young and full of myself (not a lot has changed); I walked right on in like I owned the place. I was met in the kitchen by Mrs. Claus and Martha Stewart all rolled up in the same person. She started with the usual. Her name was Marie, her husband was Ian. Could I track a wounded bear? Was I afraid of bears (not bloody likely I believe I responded)? Could I clean fish, clean a moose; clean a bear, clean boats? Etc..Etc. It sure sounded like a lot of cleaning too if you asked me. Her last question kind of threw me for a loop though. She looked me up and down appraising the cocksure punk who stood before her and asked "so Greg why should I hire you"? Though I was caught off guard, and yet without missing a beat I replied "because I will be the best damn staff you have ever had."

It wasn't until years later that I found out that it was those words that got me the job. I was too start that day so I went and got my stuff and moved into the staff quarters above the kitchen. One thing about living there I often awoke to the smell of bacon frying and the sound of laughter as Ian and Marie prepared the food and started their day with loving each other.

My own parents were very subdued in their displays of affection. Subdued was not a word you could have used to describe Ian and Marie. You could easily turn a corner and bump into them stealing kisses or watch Ian chase

Marie around the pool table playing grab ass. Theirs was the kind of love that was pure, light, fun, yet deep and true. Definitely one of a kind. We all should be as lucky as too love like Ian and Marie.

Now don't think I am speaking ill of my folks, their love was as real as it gets and it survived for over 30 years. After my dad passed away my mom was like half a heart going through the motions of life. The miracle of Ian and Marie was that they lived their love like it was the day after their first date everyday that they were together. It was amazing really and I quickly became a part of their extended family and I cherish the good times at Deer Trail Lodge.

# 28

Once I asked Ian in one of our more philosophical conversations, one that did not involve discussing the merits of various bear baits. As I set it up I am sure that you will have no trouble imagining the scene Dear Reader.

Two guys sitting on a west facing porch, as the sun goes down. The glow of the setting sun only barely interrupted by the glow of a couple of lit pipes. The only sound on the becalmed night air is the periodic hiss of the next beer opening and the tiny satisfied sigh that accompanies that first cold sip.

The younger turns to the older and without world weariness and in innocence asks "How he knew?". How he really knew in his heart of hearts that Marie was the one for him.

"She told me she was the one mate, with her kiss".

He drew on his pipe and let his silence be his punctuation.

It sure took a lot of years for me to learn what it was that he meant by that. Even now I can so clearly remember that kiss. The kiss that told the final story to my heart. It threatens to burst from my pencil and leak all over the page so let me tell it to you now.

The urge to kiss her grew all day like a living thing inside my chest and as it grew so did the guilt of yesterday, magnified a hundred fold no a thousand fold, with each beat of my heart. Her eyes were bright and her cheeks were flushed and rosy. Her lips were parted, and I could see just the tip of her tongue between them. This time I could not stop myself. I leaned very slowly towards her, treating her gently and giving her every opportunity to pull away from me. She did not move away but her shining expression turned slowly to one of apprehension. She stared into my eyes, as if she was seeking some kind of reassurance.

When our lips were an inch apart, I stopped and it was she who made that last move and brought our lips together.

At first it was soft, just a mingling of our breath, then it became harsher and more urgent. For a long heart stopping moment we devoured each other and her mouth tasted soft and sweet like ripe fruit. Then suddenly with a huge effort of will I broke the kiss. I closed my eyes and gripped her hand tightly, both fighting and savouring the pleasure of her soft touch. I drew her in again nonetheless. Almost as if she can read my mind her lips brush my cheek. When I open my eyes hers are only inches away, hazel and wide, full of curiosity. She closes them as I lean down and press my lips to hers, sending a thrill of heat through me.

From the first moment it is a knowing kiss, not the timid taste of strangers, it does however hold the self assurance of lovers who know each other. Her tongue is warm, her lips cool. My senses reading every curve, every contour of her body.

I slip my hand into the small of her back, and for a moment I kiss her as I truly want too and the passion behind the kiss she returns dissolves the world around us. As she kisses me I feel something shift deep within my soul, a heavy door creaking slowly open and whatever that door threatens to release is too powerful for the moment, too powerful to set free here. So again I break the kiss.

Weeks later during a round of "tell me something I don't know" she asked me if I remembered our first kiss. Immediately the warmth spread out from my heart. How can I answer that? YES!!! I have thought about it a million times, in a way that is not even a thought but a constant awareness of how her mouth opened to mine, the coolness, the knowingness, how from that moment on I was hers completely.......I simply said yes I remember, let me tell you a story.

# 29

Uou know what Dear Reader? Never in my wildest dreams, though had I longed for love, believed in love, wanted so badly for true love to be mine, did I ever think that I would have "that kiss". I don't know.

Since I was a young boy I had read the stories, watched the movies, the kiss that woke a sleeping princess, and the kiss that through its magic turned a frog into a prince. Princess Buttercup's kiss realized the dread pirate Roberts was really her Wesley returned to her. Patrick Swayze's kiss goodbye at the end of ghost. Underneath a pine tree, deep in the bush our kiss was all that and so much more, whether I believed in it or not.

It was a kiss that changed my life. One kiss, really just two lips touching and my life went completely off the rails and veered off in a new direction.

Part of the reason I didn't have much faith in me having one of those magical kisses was my track record. You Dear Reader have read about a hurried peck on a dark night in behind cabin 4 at summer camp. Also you've read of a kiss cajoled out of me by moonlight. Let me use Christine to further my case for poor first kisses.

Christine may figure more prominently a little later on so I don't want to give away too many details. It does however seem appropriate to tell this part of the tale here to give you Dear Reader the gist of how lucky I was in the first kiss department. You may not know some of the people coming up and I don't want to take the time to introduce them here. Trust in the fact Dear Reader that I will get there.

Now maybe I am a slowpoke, it is however important to me to be really sure about things before I commit myself to anyone or anything. So similarly to Tanya after about 3 weeks of dating Christine mentioned to a mutual friend of ours, who mentioned it to Nigel, that she was curious when I was going to get around to kissing her.

Nigel was very serious about his assigned role of wingman and he felt it was his duty to make sure that Christine and I were in a situation where our first kiss couldn't help but occur. Being the kind of friend that he is Nigel promptly invited us over to Christine's house to watch a movie. I think that he neglected to tell Christine that we were coming.

Christine had a roommate at the time and soon after we arrived Nigel asked Heather if she wanted to go upstairs to "talk", leaving Christine and I alone to "watch" the movie. Heather was in every sense of the world a "big" girl and she had a crush on Nigel. I cannot stress enough how the two hours Nigel spent upstairs was the truest definition of taking one for the team (no not that get your mind out of the gutter). I will say it here again Heather may have been the biggest girl I have ever met personally, she was easily over 400 pounds.

Nigel who was definitely not short on charisma (just short), used his own debonair nature to entertain Heather just to provide the alone time the above mentioned first kiss needed to occur.

You know, come to think of it, I am not sure if I ever thanked him properly because of the ensuing chaos. Oh well thanks buddy, not that it means much now.

Christine was wearing "comfy" clothes and was mortified by us "just showing up". I just told her that she looked beautiful and as far as I was concerned that was the truth. Other than Chantelle (she figures in this tale later) up to this point Christine was the most beautiful girl I had ever seen and I am not too embarrassed to say she intimidated me.

Nigel the mastermind of the whole evening tried to soothe her with platitudes such as "won't be staying long" and "just happened to be in the neighbourhood". Once Christine was sufficiently calmed Nigel smoothly and swiftly extradited himself and Heather from the situation, leaving Christine and myself alone on the couch.

The next two hours passed as if they were but a moment. Talking, laughing, I am sure you get the idea. Heathers shifting weight upstairs alerted us to the possibility that they could be returning downstairs at any second. I once again became aware of what the expressed intent of tonight's little trip was. Not wishing to face Nigel's ire, but also not able to find the "perfect" opportunity for a kiss, I gave up.

As Nigel came downstairs I grabbed my coat and headed for the back door.

Eyes lit up like a little kid that had just been handed an ice cream cone, Nigel asked "So how was it? Was it worth the wait?". My slumped shoulders and downcast eyes did not please him as I am sure you can imagine Dear Reader and he started to push me back into the house. Hissing he said "Get in there and do it god damn it!". I mustered all my courage and I ran back over to where Christine was lying on the couch. Allowing barely a second for confusion to set in, as to why I had reappeared in her living room, I grabbed the sides of her head and I kissed her deeply. Heart in my throat and shakily I broke the kiss and bolted for the back door. I know very chivalrous eh? Nigel told me later that I was as white as a ghost as I stammered "Let's go, let's goo!!!" I was unable to even tell him what had happened; I was so shocked by this brazen first kiss.

Nigel had a bit of a thing for my roommate at the time so with 12 beers we arrived at my apartment and Nigel was going to spend the night.

As I put my key in the lock, no easy task for my still shaking hands, the silence was interrupted by my shrilly ringing phone. Still not able to really speak, Nigel answered the phone.

It was his braying laughter that broke through my shock and filtered by his hysterical giggling I heard him say "What do you mean your lip is bleeding?"

Unfortunately in my haste to kiss her I must have banged my tooth against her lip or banged her own tooth against her lip. Either way her lip had split a bit and she was bleeding. This made for a very memorable, if not embarrassing first kiss. This also set me up for the expected vampire jokes for the next few months from our friends once the story got out.

So as you can see it was against a backdrop of first kisses like this that I shared the unexpected final kiss that would change my life.

If I was sitting on that porch today, pipe lit, beer in hand, watching the sun go down I would be able to say "yup, I know exactly what you are talking about when you say, it was in her kiss that she told me."

# 30

eer trail was a great place to cut your teeth in the resort industry. It was a small operation, 9 cabins, 12 boats and the main lodge. We have previously discussed some of my contributions to the décor of the main lodge.

Ian was a good man and not afraid to get his hands dirty with the staff. I can remember one particularly bad storm, lightning flashing all around us, we struggled to bail boats side by each as the hair on our arms stood at attention from the statically charged air. A bolt crashed into the old satellite dish only a few yards from us and Ian wanted me to leave him there so he could finish and I would be safe. Many hands make light work and though we lost the front pilings of cabin 6 that night not a boat sunk. If we are summed up by the stories that people tell of us let me tell you a good one for Ian.

We heard the whooping and hollering from quite a ways out. One of our guests was excitedly and rapidly coming into the dock. Deer Trail had a policy that no boat should ever hit the dock without someone there to greet it. From the far end of camp I raced down to the dock and while I was tying up the boat our guest held up a beautiful 54 inch Muskie. You may think that is a bit of a stretch to call a fish beautiful but she truly was. Only the females get that big in case you are asking yourself how I determined her gender. This fish glistened with a shade of silver that I had never seen before or since, all down her blood line ran the deepest colour of sunset salmon. She was a remarkable trophy fish.

Her beauty aside, she presented a real problem, though she was a trophy by every definition, it was 4 days until Muskie season opened.

Ian saw red. I had never seen him as furious as he tore up one side of our guest and down the other.

Now in case you didn't know, and I feel it safe to assume that you don't, I mean what are the chances that an ichthyologist would have survived the zombies and would be the one to find this manuscript.

The Muskie or Muskellunge is the second largest fresh water game fish, only the Sturgeon gets larger. Anglers used to refer to the Muskie as the fish of a thousand casts and for good reason, this fish was notoriously difficult to catch. For all of its size this fish was also extremely delicate, the slightest disturbance of the protective slime coating often proved fatal to the fish.

This particular beauty was used rough and on her last legs. Ian grabbed her from the guest and started emergency first fish aid. If you ever need to resuscitate a fish, please make sure you use a side to side motion because a forward, backward motion can drown the fish. Yes, drown the fish.

I know what you are thinking, don't argue with me, you absolutely can drown a fish. Oh, Dear Reader roll your eyes all that you want. Why pick now to argue? I have espoused anti-environmentalism and anti-liberal views and you pick now? Well you have no leg to stand on because whether you believe it or not you can drown a fish.

Look, I am sorry. When I know I am right I can get a little bit belligerent. Let's just move past this. Let us put it behind us so to speak. How about this? To make it up to you, let me tell you a story about her. I know I am shamelessly baiting you to continue reading but puhhhleease! See I am not above begging. I know now that you are essential to this whole process. I need you. I started this to preserve my sanity but without you this whole thing will have been for naught.

So not a dream but a story, this happened, I will leave it for you Dear Reader to decide which of my dreams are based in reality.

Do you want a quick story where I use a whole bunch of adjectives to describe the way she looked like, beautiful, gorgeous, radiant, stunning, and amazing? Should I use a few more to describe how I felt, awestruck, paralyzed, joyful, amazed? I could throw in a few more to describe her deeply pooling, captivating eyes and brilliant, dazzling, sparkling smile? Employ some flowery words about how she has captured my heart and inspires me to be a better man? Should I talk about how I fell and am hers for as long as she wants me or does that just make me a dork?

Does that really give you a feel for her? No, I don't think so. Does it let you in and help to illustrate how an us became a we? No, not really. So for this tale I will need to give you a bit of a set up.

I love bears! In fact it might even be safe to say I have a little bit of an obsession with bears. I passionately hunt bears; I even have a bear tattooed on my right leg. I love bears! Ok, I think you get the idea.

Early on, before I was willing to admit to myself that I loved her, but after I knew that I wanted too. I invited her to come to the dump with me. It may not seem like the most romantic place to take a girl but give me some credit, it wasn't like I sidled up to her and whispered in her ear "hey baby, want to go to the dump with me?" I needed to take the trash and dumps are a great place to see bears, ergo I love going to the dump. Since I was starting to enjoy our time spent together, I wanted her to come with me.

The crux of the story occurred after we had actually arrived at the dump. My hand was laid out next to me almost in the middle of the trucks bench seat. When I looked down her hand was only inches from mine. The urge was damn near overwhelming, the urge to just raise up my hand, reach over and take her hand in mine. It would have been so simple really, remember it was just inches. Hit a pothole my hand bounces up and comes to rest on hers, step one. Step two, gauge her reaction. A simple plan, all the reasons not too and the desire too created a cacophonous argument within my head.

This tumult was interrupted by her yelling excitedly "There!! Hey Greg there's a bear!!!"

I had to reverse the truck to pull into where the bear was. The point of the whole story is, I was so distracted by wanting to hold her hand that I missed the bear. Me! The guy who loves bears. I was so focused on wanting to hold her hand, wanting that closeness with her that I missed the bear.

Her uncontrolled enthusiasm at actually seeing a bear (she even whistled at it to see if it would come back) let me glimpse a hidden potential in her. Being nervous to hold her hand, well let's just say she was special. My life was better for having her in it. When I closed my eyes and imagined my future it always seemed better and brighter with her by my side. There ... are you happy? Let us go back to our drowning fish.

Both Ian and I worked that fish for over 3 hours, up to our shoulders in damn near freezing water. Finally she splashed from our grasp and dove for the bottom. We had saved her. Well almost, on a sad note Marie found her floating belly up a few days later out in front of cabin 4. I can only assume that she succumbed to the stress. Marie mad me promise not to say anything to Ian because she knew that he would be devastated. I never did.....unless of course, that is you Ian that has found this manuscript then weeelll...... "Hey look to your left a deep fried mars bar!"....ha, ha...classic misdirection. As I tell this tale I realize that my life has not been full of happy endings. My time at Deer Trail was no different.

# 31

efore I write what could be a melancholic chapter and since I have set the precedent let me describe for you the typical bear hunt here. Of all the things that I am trying to convey this is one that I need to get just right.

I saw a blackish blur out of the corner of my eye and my heart starts to beat a little faster. The bear stood half in shadow, wriggling his nose as it snuffled the air. Its head was held high, suspicious and alert. The soft breeze was quartering between me and the animal, but every so often a wayward gust gave him the faint whiff of humanity causing his apprehension. The wind must have changed because the bear lowers his head and takes some tentative steps towards the bait. I wait for him to come within range. Abruptly the bear comes to a halt, quivering with tension and I think to myself "damnit, the wind must have changed again. He doesn't like something." At that moment the bear bolts, he streaks back the way he has come and disappears in the heavy brush. Frustrated but knowing that he will be back I settle against the tree to wait. A woodpecker lands next to my stand and the chipmunks' race back and forth from the bait grabbing little pieces of dog food. The heat from the sun causes me to drowse as the forest life unfolds before me.

Suddenly without warning, the bear stepped out from the deep cover and the late evening sun gleams on his silky coat. My breathing quickens with excitement. After so many bears it is ridiculous that I should get so worked up hunting this regal animal; however the earlier failure had served to heighten my anticipation. Added to that was that peculiar passion that drives a true hunter and this bear was a beast, 48 inches at the shoulder at least.

My forefinger rested lightly next to the trigger as I came to full draw. I would not fire until the bear came to a standstill. Even at his walking pace it would make the shot uncertain. I have to place the arrow precisely, to kill swiftly but at the same time to inflict the least possible damage to the pelt.

To that end I use 2219 aluminum arrows with solid forged Montec G5 heads, ones that would not expand on impact and open a wide wound channel, nor rip a gaping hole in the skin as they exited. These solid arrows would punch a smaller hole and the taxidermist would be able to repair it to invisibility.

I felt my nerves screw up as I realized that the bear was not going to stop in the open and I was fast losing my light. He was making steadily for the opposite side and more cover. Just before disappearing into the cover he changed his mind and bent to sample the bait. Standing broadside to me, he began to nibble on the cake icing. His head was screened, however the shoulder was exposed. I could make out the clear outline of the blade beneath the glossy black fur. The bear was angled slightly away from me, in the perfect position for a heart shot, low in behind the shoulder. Unhurriedly I lined him up in my peep sight and pressed the trigger.

At the bows muffled whip crack the bear bounded high, coming down to touch the earth already at a full run. Like a laser rather than a battle axe the solid arrow had not bowled the bear over. Head down, the bear dashed away in the typical frantic reaction to an arrow through the heart. He was dead already; he was just running on the last remnants of blood and adrenaline.

"Now the real work begins" I think to myself as with shaking fingers I try to light a cigarette. 10-20 minutes later I hear the familiar and unique death moan of a bear and I am amazed because it sounds to be much farther away than you would think a heart shot bear could run. Having had much experience I know that the only thing you can expect with a bear is the unexpected they are unbelievably tough animals. I once tracked a bear 130 yards past the point where the last of his intestines came out.

Knowing now that it is safe to go in and get him I don't bother waiting for help and start in on the blood trail. Without experience I wouldn't recommend this to you, bears are incredibly intelligent and the will hold their breath when they hear you coming before they charge, I have a friend who lost his shoulder this way. Following the blood trail he reached under a spruce bough where the bear was holding his breath. Taking his shoulder in his mouth the bear tore off his arm. Confident that the bear was dead I proceeded to start to track him. Since most bears are shot late this is almost always done by flashlight and it behoves you to leave a trail you can follow back or else you might get lost. Bears are remarkable and they can slow down their heart rate so the blood they leave could be very minimal and it takes a practiced eye to be able to pick it out from the various things that litter the forest floor.

Never knowing the bear to take the easy path I track the bear over and under fallen logs across a stream up and down hills, my back is aching from hunching over and my clothes are sopping with both sweat and forest moisture. Perseverance pays off as the black shadows next to a pine coalesce in to the crumpled form of a bear. Elation washes away my body's complaints and out he is hauled. I won't describe what goes into cleaning a bear here I just wanted you to get a feel for the hunt, before we go back to Deer Trail Lodge.

# 32

Saturday was our change over day. This meant that last weeks guests left in the morning and this week's guests arrived in the afternoon. My mornings were spent cleaning boats and getting everything ready for a new week. As our first guests arrived I would quickly help them unload their gear and then usher them down to the docks. Once we arrived at their boats I would give my prepared spiel about life jackets, kill switches, safety kits and slot sizes, 18-23 inches for Walleye had to go back, one over, three under, 27.5 to 35.4 for Northern Pike and no Muskie under 52 inches. It is amazing to me that I can still remember the rules for that lake. After the customary cracking of a few bad jokes our guests were ready to enjoy their week in the Canadian wilderness.

As was also a custom, Ian and Marie would walk arm in arm down the hill, smiling and laughing as they approached to see our guests and introduce themselves. This particular Saturday was no different than any other. As Ian and Marie came closer I caught out of the corner of my eye that Marie had stumbled and Ian seemed to be supporting her. They kept coming though, smiling until they reached the end of the dock.

Turning to greet our guests Marie just collapsed and fell off the dock into the water. Immediately Ian and I jumped in after her, we lifted her up and the guests helped her onto the dock. At that moment we didn't know it but Marie was dead before she hit the water.....massive stroke. All we knew was that she wasn't breathing and we took turns performing CPR throughout the hour it took the ambulance to arrive.

Today I can imagine how Ian felt losing the person who completed him. To feel whole and then in the blink of an eye, not to be. I had watched my mother for years try to muddle through life without Dad. I get it now. Did you know Dear Reader that I was there the night my Dad died? That's a story for later.

That gorgeous June day, standing on the dock, surrounded by bewildered guests and ambulance attendants, that was the first time I ever had to watch a heart break.

It is something that haunts me even now. You would think the image of a baby in one of those forward backpack things devouring his own mother's breast as she wildly screams. Her maternal instincts overpowering her own instincts for survival, finally succumbing to the horror of the situation and the light of lucidity going out of her eyes and she begins to dance and cackle madly.

That should be the stuff that haunts me, in its own way it does but alas not like some other stuff. When Ian realized that Marie was dead, you could see the pain crawl and creep slowly up each weathered line of his face, like a stone chip spreading and spider webbing a windshield. Following a beaten path until it reached his eyes and dowsed the light within. That blank look, that crawling emptiness, destroyer of the soul, left worse off than any zombie. An all consuming pain worn on every inch of his face.

Horrors we can become accustomed too, I can remember stories of Germans who during the height of the holocaust were so used to the stench of burning bodies that they didn't even notice the smell anymore. Fathers during Stalin's purges denouncing their own sons, knowing full well that they were condemning them to unimaginable pain and suffering at the hands of the N.K.V.D in the bowels of Lubyanka prison. Abject terror became a Soviet way of life. So as unbelievably as it may seem horror and terror can become just another obstacle in your daily life.

Even me, I am not immune. At this point when a lumbering, shambling corpse appears with only a reflex action I will dispatch it with barely (at least until recently) a thought. Did he have a family? What did she do for a living? What were their passions? Things I don't have time to factor in as I find the fastest way to sever the brain stem. I know that you Dear Reader understand what I am talking about as you have survived thus far.

Do you remember a movie called "Zombieworld"? The hero had a series of rules for zombie survival. They were cutesy things like "cardio" and they were inter-spereced throughout the movie. In reality there is only one rule for zombie survival.

1) Sever the brain stem

Nothing will drop a zombie faster.

I think all this nonchalant talk of severing brain stems really illustrates my point. Horror can become mundane if we are inundated by it; it just becomes our normal state of being. Horror can become just one more thing that we are to endure if we are to survive and horror and terror we can survive. How can one be expected to survive when love has been taken from you? Life not just endured but crushed. I saw a bleak and empty future set up shop in Ian's eyes. For months following the only light behind his eyes was fuelled by whiskey and rage. It really was all too much for the boy I was and after a month I gave my notice.

This was one of the toughest decisions of my life, I was burnt out and empty. I couldn't carry Ian, Deer Trail, and myself. Was it the right decision? I don't know. It was one more step forward and it led to my next fork in the road. The year was 1999 and my life was about to change again.

# 33

ouncing around in my typical frantic manner, 6 years earlier was my back surgery. I was able to overcome the odds and 9 months later I put on my skis for the first time in almost 2 years and I managed a few runs. I paid a heavy price for those few runs, I didn't give up however and by next season I was able to go to work for The Canadian Ski Patrol System. This is an organization of volunteers who are trained to deal with the myriad of injuries one could expect to see on a ski hill.

I can remember getting stumped at a first aid competition when the injured person in question was suffering from anaphylactic shock brought on by a peanut allergy and causing me to bring home my only silver medal in all those years. I considered this a bit of a dirty trick as it was not your usual collection of fib/tib, femur, and collar bone breaks. Muscle strains and sprains mixed in with contusions, lacerations, concussions and sucking chest wounds. In the defence of Olaf who beat me, we really did need to be prepared for anything and he guessed the condition properly. It is not like I harbour a grudge or anything, Olaf was a great patroller to work with it is just strange what it is that you remember.

Along the lines of being prepared for strangeness, once we had to deliver a baby at a ski hill. We knew what we were doing and were prepared but I'm not ashamed to admit completely disgusted by the process. It was a bloody, slimy, wrinkly, alien that screamed at us.....gross. This coming from a guy who has been up to his shoulders in bear guts. I suppose gross is a relative concept, washing one of your best friends brains out of your beard is also quite gross, believe me I know.

Let's just go back to the summer of 1999. I was 22 years old and I needed to figure out what I was going to do with the rest of my life. I loved being a hunting and fishing guide and I really wanted to be able to continue doing that, so my question dilemma was what would make a good winter job? I bet you can guess where I am going with this? Yep, you guessed it.

I made the decision that going pro was the answer. Most Rocky Mountain resorts, such as Fernie, Sunshine and Whistler hire pro patrollers from the best of the ranks of the CSPS, provided you are willing to enrol in a paramedic's course. I was well on my way to living the good life when I received my acceptance letter from Sir

Sanford Fleming College. Imagine it Dear Reader, fish all summer, hunt all fall, ski all winter and get paid. Who could ask for a better life?

After Marie's death and it became known that I was available, I was offered a lot of money to go work at a resort up near Ear Falls.

I hadn't been there long, Saturday had arrived and this was also change over day. This was a much larger operation with 5 guides, a handful of dockhands, a few cabin girls, I am sure you get the idea. The owner had asked me to put a new shifting pin in an older 40hp Evinrude motor. It was an easy task and I snapped off the cowling and popped in the pin. I yelled across the beach to one of the dock hands, to ask him if he wanted to come while I took the boat for a test drive.

At this point I was in the prime shape of my life I was 225 pounds of solid muscle and I am about 6 feet tall. I probably haven't told you that yet Dear Reader so slowly but surely you are gathering facts about me. You know, if you want to skip ahead a few pages, I wouldn't blame you. I doubt by now, that you are going to put these pages down, I mean you would have by now. So since you are committed I will endeavour to the best of my ability to make the story as entertaining as possible.

On July 21 1999, we left me yelling across the beach to a young dockhand, I think his name was Adam. I wanted to see if he wanted to come on a boat ride. Being done whatever it was that he had to do, he agreed to come along. I just had to put the motor on the boat and we would be good to go. The boat was new to us and this quick run would determine if the shifting pin would hold and then the boat would be ready for the incoming guests.

It was one of those days that make you really love the month of July. The temperature was just right around 25 degrees Celsius or 80 degrees Fahrenheit. Since most of our guests at resorts were American we needed to know how to quickly convert temperature. A simple and close way is to double the temperature and add thirty it is close enough. Tell an American that it is going to be 30 degrees tomorrow and he is liable to show up at your boat in the morning wearing a coat and a sweater. No guff.

Americans are capable of doing the craziest things. Over the years I would like to say I have seen it all, I have also learned however that as soon as I say that it usually means I am about to see something new. Here is an example.

This resort up near Ear Falls was sued because the owner did not post a warning about the black flies and mosquitoes in his brochure. No guff. This lady felt that the bugs ruined her vacation. Really.......I mean really? You come to Canada for an isolated wilderness fishing experience, in May, what the hell did you expect? Man oh man; you are surprised by the bugs, crazy eh! Well lady I am surprised you were let into Canada without your helmet. Even crazier is the fact that she won the lawsuit and her money was refunded. I am convinced the only thing crazier than Americans is their laws around suing each other; it often seems to have replaced baseball as the national pastime. Bugs are a part of life in Canada especially in May.

One time.....at band camp......no no, ha-ha. One time on a spring bear hunt in northern Quebec. I had brought the wrong face mask with me. It was open faced and after my first night in the tree it looked like I had gone a round with Mike Tyson. It was so loud sitting in the stand that you could hear absolutely nothing but the incessant buzzing.

On that particular hunt, this sow with 3 little cubs came in late on the second night. Never shooting a sow with this years cubs, I was treated to quite a show. I watched these youngsters play with the pails of bait while mom knocked over the barrel. One of the more adventurous cubs walked up the fallen tree next to my stand, coming with only 5 or 6 feet of where I sat silently. It is experiences like this that help fuel my love of the bear hunt.

Around ten o'clock I heard the ATV, it was time for my guide to come and pick me up. I could hear the sow still off to my left crunching on the apples and cattle bones from the bait. Yelling out a warning to my guide, I urged him not to come in as there was a sow with cubs just off the site.

I began to quietly climb down from my tree stand, slowly, as the twilight continued to darken. I could just make out the guide at the mouth of the path readying the shotgun. As soon as my feet hit the ground, the sow burst out from the tag alders huffing and snorting. If you have never seen a bears bluff charge, it is really something else to see. If you have been on the receiving end of a bears bluff charge you will agree with me, it is terrifying enough to turn your knees to jelly. Give me a zombie horde any day.

I froze and stood stock still. It seemed like only inches but mere feet separated us. I could see, smell and feel her breath. The twilight was illuminated by the fierce determination in her eyes, a steadfast resolve to protect her own. I was face to face with a mother's rage in its purest form. I had seen my own mother's rage a time or two. You should have seen the look in her eyes when in a fit of 15 year old anger I called her a "bitch" to her face. This was way different, this was primal. After what seemed like hours but could only have been seconds, she whirled.

Properly chastened I grabbed my gear and headed to the ATV where my knees could finally give out as my guts turned to jelly. I bet my own mom wishes I had learned that maternal lesson about 10 years earlier.

By now Dear Reader I am sure you are used to me running off on a tangent, maybe even a tangent within a tangent. Since you are still here let us keep going.

Let us go back to that July day in 1999.

# 34

The sun was glittering off the waves and the sand of the beach was the perfect temperature to walk through as I lugged that big old motor over to the boat and pushed her in for her maiden voyage. Nothing as spectacular as breaking a bottle of champagne across her bow, just a sweating 22 year old pushing with all his might.

The motor started right up with no problems. It had just been cleaned and greased so I really wasn't surprised and we were off. Everything was going smoothly and shifted fine so I was convinced to give her my seal of approval, she was ready for guests.

As I turned to head back to camp, the world goes into slow motion for me, much like the Hail Mary throw at the end of a football movie or the bottom of the ninth homerun to win the world series, of which as we have discussed Joe Carter had brought from the realm of fantasy into reality. Where every word that is said comes out in a looong drrraaawn oout baritone.

I can feel myself falling, and hitting the water. The speed with which the water closed in around me, diving for the bottom as I thought of the propeller. The dull thud and thinking "oh thank god the boat has bumped me out of the way." Followed by "that is going to leave a bruise."

Once I surfaced I saw the boat was about 100 yards away. I assume that the dockhand had killed the motor. By the time I swam over to the boat I was extraordinarily exhausted and feeling very weak. I asked my companion to help me into the boat. He told me that I was way "too big" for him to lift so I kicked myself up into the boat. A wave of darkness washed over me and I just about passed out. I looked down and I can clearly remember being confused because I didn't own a pair of red jeans.

Putting the series of events together later, this is what we can best determine happened. Unbeknownst to anyone at camp the wood underneath the drivers pedestal seat was rotten. As I turned to head back towards camp, naturally I shifted my weight. This popped the screws out of the rotten wood causing the seat to fall over. Now when you fall it is a natural and normal response to try and grab on to something nearby. I was holding the throttle in my hand, as I fell I gunned the engine in mid turn and centrifugal force threw me out of the boat and into the water.

As I was diving down, kicking for the bottom the dull thud I felt was the propeller hitting me just above my right knee. I kicked down the blade and basically chopped out half of my knee.

Lady Luck stood by me that day though as the blade came as close as 4mm from severing my ACL and only 6mm from severing my femoral artery. Had either of these occurred, rather than me be sitting here writing this tale, I would instead have been one of the half skeletal corpses, tasked with swelling the undead horde.

The thing that saved my life was that I only spent a moment in confusion as to why I had "red" jeans. Almost immediately it was like a switch flipped in my mind and it was like I went on automatic pilot. I could only compare it to a solider that reverts to his training once the bullets start flying. Everything I had ever learned with the ski patrol was at the forefront of my mind.

Though not nearly as impressive as I am going to portray it, but it is my tale right? Sooo.....if you would envision The Incredible Hulk for the next part of this tale.

Flush with first aid knowledge, I ripped off my shirt.... RRRAAARRRR!! ...and made a pressure bandage out of it. It was quite a chore to get a T-shirt tight enough let me tell you.

I turned to the dockhand to ask if he would drive the boat only to discover that he had passed out cold into the bottom of the boat. I was able to get the boat started and headed back in to camp. He came to as the boat was nearing the beach and his high pitched screaming brought all the staff down to the shoreline.

As they all piled up on the beach I am not sure they knew what to expect from all of the dockhands screaming. A ragged hole where my knee used to be I feel safe to say was not it. One of the girls on the beach fainted dead away into the sand. There was no one to help her as it was my job to be the first aid guy at camp.

Two other guides helped me out of the boat and I started to give directions on what to do with our fainted co-worker. It was a very strange feeling, almost like being outside of yourself and yet controlling yourself at the same time. I remember asking someone to go and get my first aid kit; one of the girls ran up to my cabin while the 2 guides helped me up the ramp to the main lodge.

As I just said at this point I was kind of observing myself and fear had yet to settle in.

Again in slow motion and with perfect clarity I remember turning and seeing a river......ok not a river but a stream of blood running down the ramp. Like a dam slowly opening, slow dread started to leak in as I realized that this was very serious. I have nothing from which to draw comparisons too for you Dear Reader.

The feeling was similar to the dread I felt when I couldn't reach Sebastien or her once it was confirmed that the dead were walking.

For the first time in my life I felt the need to take a loaded rifle into the bathroom with me. I set it down muzzle up against the tub. The fact that the weapon was there gave me no comfort it just made my insides quiver. I knew I could do it, I knew I had it in me, nevertheless the prospect of having to shoot someone half sickened me. Early on it was hard to distinguish the undead from their recent humanity or past humanity. I can remember praying as I splashed cold water on my face that regardless of what the future might hold that I would not have to defend myself from other human beings. I asked that all my enemies be obvious, so that when the shooting was all over, I would have no doubts and no reason to feel any guilt. I was very much aware of the multiple ironies of both my position and my prayer. It was the height of absurdity and yet I prayed this more fervently than almost any prayer I have ever prayed. In fact the only prayer I pray harder is this simple pray. God, I hope she is ok. I hope she has a reason to smile. I hope things work out the way they are supposed too. If you could allow me to be selfish I hope she knows how much I love her. Amen, that's it.

I had chosen the windowless downstairs bathroom and in the hallway I could hear my pup's nails clacking on the hardwood. This is the point where the importance of having solid plans comes into play and good precise plans even more so. You know the old saying, measure twice, cut once.

Slowly the knowledge settled in that once I left my home I was probably never going to return. Here I want to clarify, I am really not an adventurer, outdoorsman yes, adventurer no. my preference would be to bar the doors, board up the windows, and hope that trouble didn't come knocking. I also knew that taking action was the wiser course. Whatever might be coming I was way more vulnerable alone than with the others with whom I had planned to survive. Besides if she was out there, I had to do everything in my power to get to her. Timing is everything, poor timing to fall in love at the end of the world.

While splashing my face with cold water, I reached over and moved the rifle lest something burst through the door and grab it. With such a bizarre precaution already second nature, mere hours into this new reality. I was starting to think that I must have lost my mind, maybe in my race to safety I had left sanity behind me in the dust. Perhaps I had journeyed so far from rationality that I couldn't even pack my stuff. Head full of these thoughts, I washed my hands.

Before we load the car together, I suppose I should back track a bit yet again. You Dear Reader know a bit about my childhood, even less about my teenage years, almost nothing about my twenties and if you did the math from my birth date that I am in my thirties. I still have so much to say, I feel like there is so much more to tell you.

Despite my prayers, I have never been what you could call a religious man. I have no problem believing in a power greater than myself however. I believe in concepts like karma and I believe part of us lives on after we die. Not the shambling brain consuming part but an essence of who we were.

That being said the strict dogma of religion; I have a hard time with. Bread turning to flesh, wine to blood, crusades, jihad, "the devil made me do it!" poppycock at it's best.

So I guess what I believe is that our impact on others is best how we live on. How we carry ourselves is what matters and our efforts to leave a positive footprint on the lives of others. Oh shit, here we go with the footprints again, no tirade this time I promise. Who we are is the sum of our experiences. If we can try to bring a positive experience into someone's life then we live on as they live on and impact others. If it helps you to visualize think of it as I virus of the human spirit. The way we behave determines whether or not our total impact is positive or negative.

To attempt to explain a belief system that took a lifetime to develop may not be possible in just a few lines, so permit me please to use Larry as an example, because you are basically familiar with his story.

The experiences I shared with Larry helped to shape who I am, to further this point let me use one of my foster kids as an example. Sitting in the tree next to me his eyes got as big as saucers as he realized that the 2 yearlings had come in to eat "Oh, my god, Greg he whispered it's a bear." The first time he had ever seen a bear in a wild and it was a direct result of the skills that Larry taught to me. So if this experience helps to shape him into who he is, then Larry lives on in them, whether they know it or not and just assume it was me. Someone had to teach me right?

# 35

*I* am completely lost, "fuck it has to be here some-place?" "Damn it all these trails look the same!" "What kind of fucking instructions are; look for the fallen log, we are on a lake for gods sake?" I ranted and ranted because I was lost. Trying my best to be im-pressive all I had managed to do was get us lost.

I poured the bait out onto an old tree stump and we headed back down to the boat. When she lost her footing I caught her and we rested on the shore by the boat.

What were we doing? This is insane, it can't possibly work. Normal sane rational thoughts, all thrown out the window each time that her lips touched mine.

We were well past the point where each and every kiss was sweet and full of the ripened newness and the promise of early love. Yet I still hungered for each and every touch of her lips.

As the water lapped at the shoreline, I held her close, I kissed her deeply, we talked and I fell just that much more.

Time plays a nasty trick on new loves. Time turns the hours to minutes and the minutes to seconds because this happens it makes our time spent together that much more precious.

This is the day that we crossed a threshold together.

I had to admit to myself that she frightened me. I had been attracted to women before.....hell I am a guy after all. We shared something that day and I couldn't stop thinking about it. For a time all we had was each other, and for a time it seemed like that was all we would ever have again. Each other. Without a word, on the breath of a kiss we were linked, then and there. Silly eh?

It is amazing to me how people can connect. This magical thing called chemistry. I realize that it was all in the context of that place, fallen log, moss covered rock, water lapping gently, and a place where the normal rules can't apply. A place where we can't hide from each other. She shyly asks me to look into her eyes and I am struck by what I see, I am happy, deliriously so. She has validated my quest, my search for love and my belief in its primacy.

This time was a gift an opportunity that I don't want to squander. I think she realized it all first. I think she wanted me to come to this moment because she knew. She was definitely brighter than me. .... God I love this woman. Though irrelevant from where I sit now it needs to be said.

Let us go back to that perfect July day not too hot, not too cold, it was just right.

# 36

Surrounded by panicking employees we don't find Goldilocks, we have me.

I had for the first time in my life just confronted my mortality as I watched my life's blood run in a rivulet down the ramp. After the fear or dread or doom or whatever word you want to use to describe the feeling passed. I really felt more of a curious resignation to the fact that given the circumstances of my injury, and our level of isolation I just might very well die. I sure didn't want, later in life maybe but then I wanted to live very badly.

Pain broke the spell. The hypnotizing stream of blood no longer held any sway over me.

I decided that rather than go all the way up to the main lodge to treat my wound it was the wiser course to load me into the boat, we had 40 miles to travel to get to the landing. We chose an 18 footer with a large casting deck that I could be laid out on. One of the cabin girls allowed me to rest on her leg and one of the guys kept my feet together. I spent the first part of the trip trying to explain what the next step would be in properly bandaging my leg in case I passed out. A lot of the boat ride is very foggy in my memory.

I can remember at one point I had a very clear vision of Chantelle and Shay Lynne. Chantelle's one of a kind smile and Shay Lynne posing like a princess in an orange dress the day we took pictures in the park. I can remember questioning whether or not I had tried hard enough and I told the girl I was leaning against to tell Chantelle that I was sorry, I tried. I personally don't remember saying that but she told me later that was my message.

I can almost hear your exasperated sigh Dear Reader, and believe you me I can understand your consternation. I will backtrack I promise. I know Chantelle just kind of jumped into the story right out of the blue.

Reading this tale must be a little like playing with a Jack in the box. The downside being once you get around the mulberry bush you never know who is going to pop out. I can hear you asking yourself "what about Tanya?" shouting, "This sucks hey mister I am so confused!" Bear with me; I will try to wrap up this package as neatly as possible for you. It just might take a bit before I can get back to Tanya and introduce you to Chantelle.

There is also Christine......oh wait.....you kind of met Christine when I cut her lip, there will be more about her I am sure. Of course this story wouldn't be complete without mentioning my wife as well.....oh shit. I have gone and done it now, it is almost like I have stirred up a hornets nest. In your mind are you screaming "What the fuck! You have a wife?" I can see why your wheels would be spinning with questions. "This wife of yours is she the one? The love?" "Oh my god this odd little story, I have started may have a happy ending after all?" "He is married. Yay! Now I don't have to read anymore I know how it ends." Are you wiping your brow with relief?

Well I am sorry, you know how I feel about disappointing you, especially since you have invested so much time already in this tale. After my wife we will talk about Mellissa and to find out how this story ends well, you will just have to ask her. Yep, that's right, this tale ends with her and she is not my wife.

I am going to assume I have your attention again. Shall we continue Dear Reader?

So we were in the boat. That is where we left the story.

The boat was about to come up on the first stretch of white water. I can remember the boat was bucking like a rodeo bull and the spray and foam was kicked up with each crash of the bow. On one of the crashes downward, my body went upwards. Unthinkingly, really as a knee jerk (pardon the pun) reaction one of the guys grabbed my leg to stop me from going over the side. The part that sucked was he grabbed my right leg.

The searing and blinding pain brought reality crashing back in and then blessedly under its weight I passed out. It must have been the slowing of the boat that brought me out of whatever you want to call the state I was in. As we approached the dock (I really am amazed at how much the mind can remember), one of the guys in his haste to help jumped right out of the boat. He must have been just a fraction too early and I can clearly see in my minds eye his fishing hat floating on the surface of the water in the second it took for him to disappear under the water and when he came thrashing and sputtering back to the surface. I would suppose that I laughed out loud.

I can remember the stunned looks on the faces of the guests as I was unloaded from the boat. By this time I was too weak to move on my own and I needed to be carried. Ever mindful of the guides job to be upbeat no matter what, I threw out a bunch of platitudes such as "I'll be back by the end of the week.", "It looks much worse than it is.", "Catch lots of fish for me.", I am sure you get the idea Dear Reader. You can determine for yourself whether or not I was trying to be brave or just stupid. My guess is a combination of both.

I demanded once we got to the owners truck that they should put me in the box so I wouldn't bleed all over the seats. I was lifted up and laid out in the box. The cabin girl hopped in and allowed me to lean up against her.

My charming and charismatic nature kicking in on instinct (tongue in cheek, don't roll your eyes) because she was cute. She told me later that I apologized for bleeding all over her leg and I even suggested that we go for a hike when I returned to camp. Leave it to me to try and pick up a girl in the midst of dying.

We met the ambulance with about 100 kilometres to go to reach the hospital. The paramedics didn't even change my dressing so score one for the ski patrol.

After only a brief stop to accommodate on of the paramedics who needed to throw up (apparently riding sideways in an ambulance at high speeds can induce motion sickness) we arrived in Red Lake.

By this time my ability to remain conscious was severely taxed. I can remember briefly talking to my parents after I arrived at the hospital. I told them not to worry and that I was fine and that everyone was clearly overreacting to what I was now referring to as my little scratch on the knee. Shock, denial, some form of courage, I couldn't tell you. When I got off the phone I overheard one of the doctors tell either my mom or my dad that it was touch and go and that I might not make it.

It wasn't until much later that I thought about how truly horrible it must have been for my parents to have to make a 4 hour drive not knowing if I would even be alive when they got there.

I was rushed by air ambulance to Thunder Bay. When we landed the ambulance attendants didn't secure the stretcher properly and I spent the trip to the hospital bouncing around in the back of the ambulance with every corner that we took. The surgery to rebuild my knee took about 12 hours. I was sent home by air ambulance and reminiscent of 1993 I recovered at home. I had a cast from my hip to my ankle with a little window cut out at the knee so the homecare nurse could change my dressing. On a strange side note, my neighbour across the street had a huge chunk of his ass chopped out by a boat propeller. One of the many bizarre Wilde St. coincidences.

# 37

ilde St. was the street that I grew up on. It was not wild as in savage but Wilde with an "e". I have always assumed it was named for Oscar Wilde of "there are only two tragedies in life: one is not getting what one wants and the other is getting it" quotable fame. To the best of my knowledge Oscar Wilde was never on my street or even knew Dryden existed.

Wilde St. was not a candidate for a portal to a parallel universe or an alien landing zone. Although I once did see a UFO, not on Wilde St. and only in pictures after the fact but for real nonetheless. If you don't believe me I can try and find the pictures.

Are you familiar with a trail camera? This is a motion activated camera that takes pictures of animals in the bush as they walk by. A trail camera is very handy to have at a bear bait. It will tell you how many bears are coming in, what size they are, and what time they are coming in? All important questions to answer if you want to be successful in your harvest.

This particular year, 2009 I believe, a sow with cubs got irritated with my trail cam. Probably because of the flash, anyway she batted it right off the tree and it landed on its back facing the sky.

On the evening in question, the camera captured an image of a glowing red disc in the sky at 9:50pm and at 4:43 in the morning it captured a huge lighted object that was a perfect saucer shape. I am not saying that it was a space alien trying to make contact with the bears. Definitely though this was an unidentified flying object.

Ok.....I am not crazy think of it this way, if every star is a sun and every sun has planets around it, wouldn't it be the height of human arrogance to actually believe that we are the only intelligent life in the universe. In fact I would put forward the argument that the surest sign there is intelligent life on other planets would be the fact that they haven't bothered making themselves known to man.

Really Wilde St. was like any other street. The houses were nice and upper middle class. The Murray's lived to the east of us, the Bonham's of Barbie van and plastic arrow fame to the west. The Roll's lived across the street. Mrs. Wilson and Mrs. Delong, from grade 9 english, were the teachers on the street. The Roussin's, Parkin's and Labelle's lived up the hill. Mrs. Crawford was think kind old lady you could always count on for double treats at

Halloween. John the barber was her next door neighbour. Pam down the street was my first crush. There was the guy at the far end of the street who had 2 Dobermans that he never chained up, they would chase and try to bite us on our way home from school. Mr. Hughes was our streets policeman and the Zuchiatti's, Krakow's and few others rounded out the Wilde St. of the 1980's.

Pretty much sounds like any ordinary street right? In some ways you would be correct in that assumption Dear Reader. On any given summer night the sound of children playing tag, street hockey or hide and go seek could be heard, at least until the street lights came on.

Neighbours yelled out their hellos over the sound of the lawn mowers and often stopped by to "yak" over an iced tea or cold beer. The houses all had manicured lawns and neat flower beds. There were just enough dandelions to be able to go out into the yard and pick a "bouquet" of flowers for mom on a hot summer day.

It was the kind of neighbourhood where if you went away for Christmas break someone would make sure that your driveway was shovelled. If you needed to run down to the corner store for something you didn't need to lock your doors and when you returned it wasn't in the least bit strange to find your buddy waiting for you in your kitchen eating a sandwich.

I know sounds idyllic right? In the last years BZE, we were inundated with such horrifying images and ideas, a parent couldn't even send their kids to a public park to play without supervision.

In contrast the most common words heard in my house as a child were "get you butt outside and play". Often I think that a child's and more so my random and flighty nature led to my mother not knowing "exactly" where we were playing. Of course one of my mom's super powers allowed her voice to carry great distances to wherever we were playing when she needed to call us in for dinner or even just wondering where we were.

For all it's idyllicness Wilde St. also had its oddities. There was Bob Zuchiatti; he was born with an extremely rare disease, a piece of his brain was missing and although normal in every other respect he always felt like he was starving to death. All of the cupboards in his house and even the fridge had locks and chains on them. This was to protect him because as you could imagine if Bob got in he would eat and eat and never be full. I have always felt that this must have been a truly terrible way to live.

Thinking about it now I wonder if the reanimated brains of the undead suffer from some such abnormality. Bob was always on the hunt for something to eat, the zombies I have seen are always on the hunt for someone to eat. Possibly during the reanimation process that particular part of the brain doesn't get activated and the ravenous undead horde really suffers from some form of Prader Willi's disease.

Bob as you can well imagine and through no fault of his own was extremely overweight. Sometimes good questions come to me.

How is it with the copious amounts of calories the average zombie must consume that they never seem to gain any weight?

Well Bob was absolutely huge. He never really could play tag or hide and go seek with us. He did however play football when we were older and which ever team picked him just had to give him the ball and he became an unstoppable juggernaut who homed in on the opposing team's end zone. So at least for football he was a sought after commodity.

Prader Willi's is an extremely rare birth defect, though it is estimated that 1 in 15,000 used to suffer from some form of it. It does have an explanation that one can if not easily at least understand. You are born without the part of your brain that tells you when you are full thus you are starving all the time, horrible but understandable. I should add here that Bob died at 23 years of age due to a weight related heart attack far too young.

Other things that happened on Wilde St. are not as easy to explain.

Let us talk about Erin Hughes. Erin was a lot older than most of the kids on the street and so it often fell on her shoulders the responsibility of being the neighbourhood babysitter. In 1986 she developed some problems with her pancreas and had to be flown to a hospital in Winnipeg. At the same time my mom was in a different hospital in Winnipeg having 2 brain abscesses removed.

Walking the dog with my grandma who was down watching me and my sister so dad could be in Winnipeg, we noticed that the lights were on in Erin's bedroom and we could hear the music coming from her stereo. I can remember being very excited that Erin was home and I wanted to go right over and say "HI" and to see how she was doing? Grandma felt that Erin probably needed her rest and it would be better if we stopped by tomorrow.

The next day when we went over we found that the house was empty. Erin had died the night before as the result of a blood clot and surgical complications. I have always since believed that Erin came home one last time before she moved on too wherever she was headed too.

Even later on the strange sicknesses continued. When dad got sick with cancer his type of cancer only constituted 1% of all cancers, and though multiple myeloma was rare there were 3 cases on Wilde St.

When I think back on my childhood the happiest times were spent on and around Deadmans Lake and up and down Wilde St. We as kids didn't cross the Colonization Ave boundary; to play with the kids who lived further east on Wilde St. in fact the only kid I ever really played with from that part of town was Sharpie. The other kids from that side included Brankin (of my little horsey fame). The bullies Lafortress and Skillen and big Richard Bale a strange kid who didn't have a TV, play cards or later on go to the school dances.

These were definitely care-free and good times and with all the effort that went into my upbringing you would think that I should have turned out better.

A quid pro quo here that you need to know Dear Reader is that my parents did the best they could with what they had to work with. I was difficult, stubborn and bull-headed, couple that with a lazy attitude and a determination to follow my heart in all things and you end up with a very difficult child to raise. I just want you to know Dear Reader that the examples I was given are beyond reproach.

I have often been overheard saying "if I can be half the man my dad was then I will have done alright with my life". I guess it would depend on who you asked whether or not they would say I have hit the mark. That being said I can't think of what I would change. The experiences that I have had have shaped who I am and for the most part I am ok with that.

Given the opportunity to ask my mother I wonder if she would say that she was proud of me or not. I can at least say with a sense of pride that I have always followed my heart, though not always to the best results, I have been true to it. My father missed some of my greatest accomplishments and failures but I would like to believe that when he passed on our slate was clear.

Let us leave this point for a bit Dear Reader and move back a few years, to a time before Ear Falls. I know I have mentioned Chantelle and I am sure you are wondering what happened to Tanya. So let's hit rewind and go back to the summer of 1996.

# 38

The summer of 1996 was a magical time, ha-ha, ok ok let's not be too sappy. It was a good summer though. This was the year that I turned 19. An advertisement in the paper let me know that a resort near Aitikokan that needed a couple to work at it. Since Tanya and I were not sure what schools we wanted to go to and where our futures were headed, we both felt that applying for this type of a job would be a great trial run for us living together. So that is what we did. We applied and got the job at the Trading Post.

The owner was a diminutive old lady who was tougher than almost anyone I had ever met up to this point. She was definitely cut straight out of the true north strong and free in this way she was much like Larry.

Betty and her husband inherited the resort from Betty's father in 1946. In 1949 her husband was killed in a float plane crash. Betty never remarried and once over the ritualistic 3:30pm gin and tonic (something she credited her longevity too, that and cooking everything in bacon grease. I am serious; I mean how could you make this stuff up and besides you haven't lived until you cook pancakes in bacon grease.) I was able to ask her why she never remarried. She told me that she never remarried because her husband completed her in ways that she did not know she needed completing in. If Betty was still around I could tell her I now get it. At the time it seemed so terribly sad and Betty and her husband joined Larry and Annabelle in the long suffering true love category.

I have mentioned that Betty was tough and I want to give you an example of her toughness and I promise that I will. First though I want to thank you for sticking with me this far. I can understand that at times this narrative has been cumbersome, disjointed and hard to follow. Bouncing from year to year and different times in my life, many different stories going on at once and they are only loosely connected at this point. By the time you set down these pages however I hope you will feel that the journey has been worth it and I also hope you will know my loves and have fondly remembered your own.

I know we all sit on a precipice. Civilization as we have known it, as I describe it here is no more. Wilde St. is truly wild. Those of us who survived are left with the unenviable burden of rebuilding a world for humanity to survive in. Our great legacy as a species will not be the fantastic machines we have built; they will rust. Mankind's greatest buildings will crumble and fall succumbing to times relentless march. Will our vast stores of music and prose live on? I doubt it. I think our greatest legacy will be that we lived, despite all of our faults. With both successes and failures we still persevered. As a species we continue on. The impact we leave behind built on a cornerstone forged by the uniquely human capacity to love.

Even as I write about people who are tough and who have inspired me, their toughness, their ability to withstand the trials and tribulations of life springs from their almost infinite capacity to love.

Let us go back to Betty now.

# 39

I may have promised you a story about Betty but as I think of our infinite capacity to love; I am struck with the knowledge that love has an infinite capacity to change us as well. Let me talk about hunting and how love changed that for me.

The stand was halfway up the lone Jack Pine tree, roughly 15 feet off of the ground. Not to protect us for a bear could climb if he was so inclined and be in the tree with us faster than we could catch our breath. Rather it was raised to provide us with a wider field of view over the bait placed below.

I had chosen the site carefully. Most important it was above the prevailing easterly evening breeze that gently wafted the scent of burning honey over the clear cut. Also it was surrounded by just enough cover to give the bear confidence in his approach.

A fallen tree weighted down the 5 gallon pail that was 20 yards away. The weight would make the bear work for the dog food, molasses, and cake icing hidden underneath.

I knew the bait was 20 yards; I had measured it with my range finder. The stand was a typical 2 man ladder stand with bench seating and less than comfortable cushioning. A brown fleece blanket that still smelled faintly of her covered our laps. My pack had some snacks, cover scent and a thermos of hot coffee for what could be a long vigil.

Both of us had brought books to whittle away at the hours until dark, but neither of us opened them. We sat side by each on the bench and I was vitally aware of our proximity to each other. I felt by now comfortable in her presence as if this was an old and often practiced custom. I smiled at the idea. I turned my head to steal a glance, which she must have anticipated because she was smiling already.

She shifted slightly, and I slid my arm through hers and grasped her hand. The trepidation at that task long gone. As I took her hand in mine I was surprised by the smooth warm feel of her skin and by the sharp emotion her touch invoked. I hadn't felt like that in a long time. We sat like that side by side, like a couple on its first date and waited for the bear to come.

Although all of my senses were tuned to the subtle sounds and signs of the wilderness all around us, my mind was free to wander around and sort through the junk of my memories.

I thought of many things in the hours that it took the sun to race across the sky and start to sink on the horizon.

I thought of other women I had known, Tanya, Chantelle, Christine. Others whom the passage of time had rendered faceless and nameless. I also thought of loneliness. In my lifetime I have learned that loneliness is the most destructive of feelings. Most of my life I have felt alone.

In all the multitude of people that filled my life, from friends and family to acquaintance and associates. I had mastered the art of being alone in a crowd.

There was really only one person with whom I was able to share all the triumphs and disasters of my life. One who had been constant in his understanding and love.

Dad had passed away years ago however and I was sick to my soul with loneliness and afraid of the greater loneliness that I knew lay ahead.

At that moment the woman who sat beside me tightened her grip on my hand almost as if she empathized with my despair. When I turned my head to look into her hazel eyes she was smiling but serious and she held my gaze without shifting or embarrassment. The sense of aloneness faded, and I felt a calmness and a peace that I had seldom felt in my life.

Outside of our tree stand, the light mellowed and flared into the soft glow of the northern Ontario twilight. It was a time of magical stillness in which the world held its breath and all the forest colours, were richer and deeper. The sun sagged like a wounded warrior and bowed its bloody head below the treetops.

Within the tree stand she pressed her lips to mine. It wasn't our first kiss. It may not have been our hundredth kiss. Each time that her lips touched mine though it recharged my soul. It was this collection of kisses that saved my life.

Within that moment, sitting there beside her I suddenly realized that my own hunting of bears might be over forever. Like so many older hunters I had had my surfeit of blood. I loved the hunting game just as much, probably more than I ever had, but it was enough. I may have killed my last black bear, moose or caribou. This thought made me glad and sad at the same time, a kind of sweet warm melancholy that mingled well with the new emotion I had conceived for this beautiful lady who had just laid her head on my shoulder. I thought of how I would take my pleasure in the hunt through her, the way I was doing it now at this moment. I dreamt happily of travelling with her to the hunting fields of the world; Uzbekistan for the sheep of Marco Polo, the Arctic for the great white bear, The Yukon to harvest a regal and majestic monster moose and to Tanzania to fulfill her dream of shooting a big old tom leopard. These vicarious pleasures sustained me as I daydreamed.......... The light strengthened; vaguely I could make out the open window through the foliage of the ebony tree. The outline of the branch appeared slowly out of the gloom as I blinked, the branch appeared blank and my heart sank, for her sake.

I turned my head to tell her that the leopard was gone, but I never took my eyes off the branch. I held my words on my lips and I stared harder. A feeling like tiny ants of excitement crawls along my nerve endings. The outline of the branch was harder, and it was strangely thickened and misshapen.

I could just make out the blob of the dangling dik-dik carcass. Most of it had been devoured. It was a ravaged bundle of bared bones and torn skin, but there was something else hanging from the branch, a long snake like ribbon. I could not decide what it was until it curled and swung lazily, and then I realized" The Tail!, The leopards tail!" Like a picture hidden away within a puzzle, the whole jumped into focus.

The leopard was draped still on the branch, lying flat with his neck outstretched. His chin was propped up on the rough bark. He seemed to be sluggish with the weight of the meat in his belly, too lazy to move from his perch. Only his long tail swung below.

I felt her stiffen next to me as she made out the shape of the leopard. As my hand touched her arm I could feel her vibrating like the strings of a violin lightly touched with the bow.

In the golden glow of the new morning sun, the dappled savannah prince, slowly raised himself in a stretch that rippled him from tip to tail. A gaping yawn showcased his polished ivory, scimitar shaped fangs and curling pink tongue. Viscera and gore from the mangled Dik-dik was drying on his chiselled muzzle. Movements both graceful and savage, primitive and measured.

He raised himself up presenting his sweet spot.

I will her to shoot, "shoot him, and shoot him" running through my head. I longed to see his lifeless body drop from the branch. To see the unique look of ecstasy on her face that only a successful hunt can bring.

She brings the bow to full draw........and I remember where I am.

Not a tree stand waiting for a bear, not a blind in the African savannah. A beach, a lonely little beach. My personal Elysium amid destruction that would have made Shiva proud. The dead ramble, the dead rule. I have tithed in blood. A surfeit now for sure. Blood or love I have paid my share. What would I say if she appeared now? These experiences have changed us. I am not the same how could she be?

I would say "when I woke up this morning I thought of you. My thoughts full up with your beaming smile and brilliant eyes. I was swarmed with visions of the life we could have had. Happy, simple, guided by love. Looking forward to the moments spent together. Then reality crashes in. I am without you.

I hope you are smiling. I hope you are loved. I hope you are happy.

# 40

ove can make us do some strange things, I wouldn't try to excuse all my behaviours and this isn't the place or time for that. Let us Dear Reader rejoin our story with Betty.

During the late 70's, on one January day, when I close my eyes I picture it as one of those sunny, yet frost bitten days, where each bare deciduous branch glistens with a crystalline covering and each breath that you take invigourates rather than freezes your soul. A cloud of exhalation punctuates each of Betty's crunching steps through the crust covered snow.

This is the day I picture, when I imagine Betty strapping on her snowshoes and trying to stay in shape even though she is rapidly approaching her 70's. As she tells the story I can't help but picture her current incarnation of a black lab constantly by her side.

He catches a scent on the wind, and dashes off a couple of yards, stopping, pawing the snow and excitedly barking to let Betty know that he had found something interesting and she needed to come over right away to check it out.

I can picture Betty's uniquely wry smile on her face as she makes her way over to the dog.

A bear in its den.

To hear the tale from Betty she was unwilling to pass up this unexpected windfall of fresh meat. Betty hustled back to her house to retrieve her rifle and sled. Lucky for her she left a stick in the snow to mark the den or else she may not have been able to find it again.

Jamming her rifle into the mouth of the den, Betty fired 2 shots "for good measure". Then she sat down in the snow to wait for the bear to bleed out. After 20 minutes or so Betty was convinced that the bear was "done for". Why she didn't wait for the death moan I will never know. She reached into the den to grab the unlucky bruin and haul him out of the den "I knew he was a male" she says "because I listened for the mewling of the cubs". When I pointed out that she had been half deaf since the 60's, she gave me her knowing wink and said "I'd a been surprised by her skirt then eh!" laughing at her own joke, she continued her tale.

Gripping the bear firmly about the head, she went to heave once and quickly jerked back her hand. Her hand had a blank space where her last 2 fingers should have been. She promptly picked up her rifle and shot the bear 2 more times. She tie doff the stumps of her fingers and plopped back into the snow to wait another 20 minutes, she was unwilling to abandon her meat. Using the stick she placed in the snow as a marker Betty poked the bear until she was satisfied that the bear was well and truly dead.

She then proceeded to haul out the bear, load him on the sled and drag him back home. During the process of cleaning the bear Betty was able to retrieve her fingers, which she pickled and placed in a position of honour on the mantle above the fireplace. I have seen them. I wonder when the dead awoke did those fingers begin to twitch and swim in that old pickle jar.

I arrived at the trading post about 4 weeks before Tanya was able to get there. Our cabin was on top of a hill and was west facing so we got all the sunsets. It was a one room cabin, with a fridge, stove, kitchen table, counter and a big old brass bed.

After about 2 weeks of being there I noticed that this chipmunk was eating my fruit loops. I immediately began to formulate a plan to kill the little bugger. I was slowly moving a pile of fruit loops closer and closer to my foot until BAM! I could stomp him. I want to be clear here, I was only resorting to this level of violence because I was unable figure out how he was getting in to the cabin. The little bastard.

You may think that my reaction is extreme, it was however 40 miles by boat to the nearest store and this made cereal fairly precious. I was also determined to have our cabin rid of "vermin" before Tanya arrived.

A funny thing happened.

One day while sitting still and waiting patiently for the little arsehole to get close enough for me to unleash one more stomping attack. He gathered up some fruit loops hopped over on top of my foot and just started munching away. After getting over my initial shock at his audacity I had to admit to myself that he looked kind of cute. I watched him for a while, my murderous rage forgotten it became a challenge for me to see how close I could get him to come and within a matter of days he was coming up into my hand. A few days more and I could carry him around and by the time Tanya arrived my shirt pocket was full of fruit loops and little "hook" as he came to be known, could be found riding around on my shoulder or in my shirt pocket.

His habit of riding around in my shirt pocket was almost the death of him. When Tanya's surprise early arrival led to a bear hug of epic proportions, only a quick squeak saved him. The shriek and look of abject terror on Tanya's face was worth every second of the broken hug.

Neither Tanya nor Hook ever fully recovered from the trauma of that first meeting and they tolerated each other for the summer with thinly veiled animosity. Hook had taken in the week leading up to Tanya's arrival to spending his nights perched at the foot of bed on the brass.

The first night when Tanya tried to crawl into bed with me hook raised such a ruckus that I quickly realized that

I had the world's first and probably only chipmunk body-guard. Hook was my constant companion that summer.

I want to break here for a moment to talk about the professor. Professor was quite a character; he had a permanent cabin on the lake and was the only other male that spent the summer there. It was quite natural that we were to become friends. I spent many an evening on his deck, watching the lake as the sun went down behind us. We would discuss everything. The professor was polish and very old fashioned his affectionate pet nickname for his wife was "Weike" which sounds nice until you realize it is polish for mule. It was always said with affection in his voice however their relationship was not the type I wanted so I never really took any of his advice when it came to Tanya. He would say things like "Weike, I am peckish fix me a sandwich" or once when she returned to the states for a week, the cabin was in a shambles, when I commented on the mess he replied "I could not manage more than one Weike so there is no one here to clean" had I have tried that shit with Tanya I would have joined an elite group "The Castrati". You would think that by the mid 90's such outdated attitudes would be extinct but here they were right in front of me alive and well. Even Larry who was much older than the Professor never objectified women in that way.

That put aside however I have met many people over the course of my life whose views, beliefs and personal behaviour have not quite matched my ideals. Each time I have endeavoured to find the similarities rather than focus on our differences. To search out the good in them and to look for the ways that they can positively add to my life. It is in this way that I have been able to become friends with vegetarians, liberals and even Frenchmen during my life.

Though most might consider the Professor a cave man when it came to his treatment of women, did however have fascinating tales to tell.

During World War 2 as a member of the polish underground, he was captured and torture by the Gestapo not only once but twice. Daring rescues saved his life but his hands sported the damage caused by the thumb screws as proof.

After escaping Poland just ahead of the Red army he completed his education and worked as a political science professor at Cambridge, Yale and he ended his career as the head of political science at Stanford. He wrote 2 books; one about the Warsaw uprising and "Death in the Forest" the definitive work on the Katyn Forest massacre.

During World War 2, 25,000 polish officers were executed in the Katyn Forest. Killed with German bullets yet tied with Russian ropes. It was a mystery who was responsible. With the Soviets laying the blame at the feet of the SS and vice versa when the mass graves were discovered in 1943.

Through very diligent research the professor determined that blame for the massacre lay with the occupying Red Army and was ordered by Lavrenti Beria then the head of the NKVD, which was the precursor to the KGB.

With the collapse of the Soviet Union on December 26 1991, the fledgling Russian democratic government in an attempt to show that they were more transparent and wanting to ease tensions with former eastern bloc nations and show the world that they had changed. Admitted to and apologized for the Katyn Forest massacre. This had the dual effect of both vindicating all of the professor's hard work, while at the same time rendering it obsolete.

Part of my fascination with the former Soviet Union can be directly traced to the Professor.

The professor was also an advisor to both President Carter and President Reagan, so he also had interesting insights into the inner workings of the White House and unique personal insights into the personalities behind the Presidents.

A 19 year old kid and a cranky octogenarian sitting on a porch as the sun goes down on a secluded Canadian lake, solving all the world's problems and fixing our relationships over a scotch on the rocks and as twilight descends our faces illuminated intermittently by the faint glow of our fine Cuban cigars. Life was simple then. I think the simplicity of that life is what motivated me to seek it out again so much later on.

# 41

*J*ust because we talked about fixing our relationships does not mean that either of us considered
our relationships fraught with problems. I figured
I was going to spend the rest of my life with Tanya. So we
talked more about realistic obstacles to our success. In
retrospect the professor called what was about to happen.
I guess it is safe now to admit that he was right. I assume
he is lumbering and lurching around Washington state
and his lack of higher brain function, won't allow him the
smug satisfaction, that I am sure he would get from my
admitting he was right.

That summer holds its own beauty for me and a very
special place in my memories. I spent that summer day
in and day out with Tanya by my side. We worked side by
side day in and day out and we returned to our one room

cabin to spend our nights. We never fought, not once. We held hands on our deck smoking cigars as the sun went down, we talked about the things that we wanted out of life and sometimes saying nothing just being comfortable in each others presence and the silence. We spent time off hiking through the bush and we even discovered and ancient Sioux encampment where we collected pottery shards some of which turned out to be over 700 years old. As far as finding things go it was a chance discovery by Tanya that changed our relationship forever.

I returned one day to find Tanya standing in the middle of our cabin, hand on her hip and a slightly cross look on her face. Using a tone that was both warning and daring she asked me "what are these?" I want to make it clear that I had no expectations and I am not even sure where I got them, with only a wish and a prayer had I packed them.

Seeing Tanya there with her hand on her hip, scowl on her face, confronting me with a handful of condoms, brought full rouge to my cheeks. I stammered out some embarrassment filled response, something like "better safe than sorry" or at least as equally lame. Tanya and I regularly discussed sex, if you remember she had presented me with a list that ranged from the "bent over the kitchen table for breakfast" mundane to the "as a home video of our vacation to show our friends and family" exceptional. Based on our level of trust and caring I seriously doubt "better safe than sorry" was really what she wanted me to say.

She stormed out of the cabin and left me to stew in my "oh shit, what have I done" frame of mind. I am sure Dear Reader you can imagine the thoughts racing through my mind as I held my head in my hands and contemplated spending the next few months "trapped" in this cabin with a very pissed off Tanya. Can you see me passionately bent over as if praying with hands clasped rocking with a little chipmunk on my shoulder?

After what seemed like hours but was probably closer to 40 minutes or so the cabin door banged open. There framed in the moonlight, hands on her hips stood Tanya in her bathing suit. "Look you butthead" she said "I am not gonna stay mad forever, let's go down to the beach, have a swim and get cleaned up before bed". Without giving me the option to reply she left me to get changed.

I hurried down to the beach. If I pause I can still see her reflected in the moonlight as she sliced through the water. Me on the other hand with about as much grace as an epileptic elephant dived in and started to soap up.

As I lathered up my face and hair with my eyes closed, I felt a dull thwap as something wet hit me in the face. Suddenly I felt 2 hands on my sides and 2 lips moving up my neck. As she took my earlobe between her teeth and pulled her bathing suit off of my head she whispered "I am glad you are prepared, maybe it is time?" I really really want to go of on a tangent here about my time in the boy scouts but I also don't want to spoil the mood for you Dear Reader.

I wish I could adequately describe to you the fumbled, tentative passion that given only the tiniest of a crack to vent itself led to such hungry kisses in the water. This was followed by a hurried run clothes in one hand each other in the other, up the hill to our cabin. A giggling race that ended in a tumbled mess on our bed. The soundtrack being an angrily chattering chipmunk angrily admonishing our choice for the whole 5 minutes I must have lasted. The accusing pile of condoms left untouched on the counter top. This really was a summer of discovery and we did our best to check off her list, exploring each other and pushing our limits. By the time fall came around we knew ourselves and each other so much better.

I can hazard a guess at what's going through your mind. Teenage lovers testing our compatibility, finding happiness in each others arms and filling our nights with passion. This story has all the makings of a true romance. Are you struggling with the desire to hear about our wedding? Trying to reconcile what you have heard up until now? How does Chantelle, Christine, my ex wife, Mellissa and most especially her, figure into this tale? Why did this teenage love not last? Well to answer you I will tell you about the day our relationship finally died.

Spending 6 months together was wonderful. After we got home there were so many people to see and so much to get caught up on, that it was about 9 days before we were able to get together and be alone.

Topless and laying on my bed Tanya began to kiss her way up my stomach, with each inch that she moved the sensation of being tickled grew until I burst out laughing. Her confused look turned to merriment and before long we were both laughing so uncontrollably that tears were streaming down our faces. Once we caught our breath, Tanya attempted to look at me seriously and this set off another round of laughter. Once we were finally able to bring ourselves under control Tanya said to me "this summer really was perfect eh?" and I agreed with her. By agreeing I realized that I was agreeing that we had done it. We had reached the pinnacle of our relationship and if we stayed together we would end up like a couple of old heroin addicts forever trying to chase the dragon. We had accomplished all that we could together and we had an opportunity to recognize it and move away from each other before we started to hold each other back and we grew to hate each other for what we had become.

The beauty of that moment is that now, well maybe not now, but up until the collapse of civilization. I was able to send Tanya a message and we would chat. I was able to be happy for her in her life, as she was for me in mine. Truth be told I have always respected Tanya's bush craft (for a girl) and I have a small place in my heart that hopes she survived the zombie apocalypse.

These insights into the reasons our relationship failed came together after years of experience. At the time it hurt. It hurt badly. Understanding it was for the best and feeling it is for the best are really two different things. It would be safe to say I have always had a bit of a disconnect between my head and my heart.

# 42

*I* see now that rather than give it to you in one lump sum near the end of my book, I have instead peppered my tale with stories of her. When last we left her, excitement had lit up her face and my world came crashing in as I realized how beautiful not just beautiful, but truly gorgeous this girl was. Her excitement was contagious and I could feel my own smile creep up onto my face. I understand you know that now Dear Reader. What you don't know is that at this time there was a fierce debate raging between my heart and my mind. How was I going to proceed?

Part of me was preoccupied with how good it would feel to hold her hand in mine. I wanted so badly to look over to see her smiling and I wanted to know that I was the cause of that smile. Another part of me wanted to give up, was burnt out, afraid of the energy and cost required to build this relationship. Having just paid Mellissa's whoring price with my heart, it was empty.

So like the left and the right, the two factions fought like members of parliament debating a budget. It was a veritable cacophony of yay's and nay's bouncing back and forth inside my skull. At this point in time little did I know that it would take a slip for me to fall.

The reason I feel it is important to illustrate this here is because throughout my life there are numerous examples of my heart over riding my head. With Tanya my head won and we were both better off for it.

Tanya has or had at least a wonderful family and the children that she could never have had with me. I never seriously considered kids of my own until I met her.

The collapse of our relationship left a real void in my life. Not only was Tanya my lover, but all through my teenage years Tanya was also my best friend. We had faced all of our struggles together, and though I could do it, I hoped, I was extremely inexperienced with facing life and my emotions alone.

It was into this bleak and melancholic landscape that a girl named Jada made an appearance. I can almost hear your resigned consternation Dear Reader. I also know that I haven't mentioned Jada at all up to this point. So yet again BAM! Another girl hits you in the face. Well, the truth is that though Jada and I had a good couple of months together, she is barely worth a footnote in the grand scheme of things. So don't get all twitter pated, some girls won't even get a mention, or maybe a few more will, so please bear with me. You will see how it all comes together, I promise.

I recently read a paper extolling both the virtues and the pitfalls of extraordinary confidence. I have always believed that it is only by taking great risk is it that we can have those great life changing outcomes. Neither good nor bad just life changing, although I doubt those who know me would support all of the risks I have taken they do define who I am today.

Let us get back to Jada though. Unfortunately at least for her, she conveniently filled a void and even more unfortunately she also fell in love with me. Dating Jada was ok; I mean I liked her fine enough. I was however completely unprepared for the girl who would soon walk into my life. That being said I doubt that anyone could ever be prepared for a girl like Chantelle.

During the winter months I supplemented my summer income by driving taxi and the odd night at the local radio station. The 2 night dj's shared an apartment and that was my second home, most of my time off was spent in their company either at the apartment or on the air.

Jp and I were able to maintain our friendship throughout the years. Pat unable to face whatever his own personal demons were decided that he didn't even want to continue trying. I will never forget Jp and I kicking in the apartment door and finding Pat in a puddle of white foamy slime. 7 empty pill bottles on the ground at his feet. Pat lived. Showing his determination on his first day pass from the hospital, he got himself a room at a local hotel and hung himself.

Cold as it may seem I have often felt that Pat was probably better off since he was so set on ending his life. One of my last memories of Pat is of him being so drunk that he couldn't get up out of his easy chair, so he shit himself right there. It was a very sad time. Jp and I drifted apart, eventually we were able to reconnect and he even attended my wedding years later.

# 43

*L*ike I just said, at that time I was I taxi driver. Believe it or not I loved it. The things you may have heard are all true, people will give you anything, TV's, VCR's (it was that long ago), jewellery and yes I couldn't even count the number of times I was propositioned to pay a fare. I had a girlfriend the whole time that I drove so I never accepted that form of payment.

One night, the spring of 1997 I believe, I was parked in front of the Kenrica Hotel when this girl, oh what a girl, in a little black dress (oh come on you know the one, every girl has one in her closet, the little black dress). So this girl in a little black dress opens the back door of my cab hops in and asks me to take her to 6 Minto place. I am amazed almost 20 years and I remember the address.

As we made typical cabbie small talk we came to the realization that her brother "pork" was a good friend of mine, noticeably relaxed as we approached her apartment building she said to me "I'm not really all that tired yet, do you want to go grab a coffee?" The thing was I did, I really wanted to continue talking with her. I called in to dispatch and since the bar rush was over I signed myself out for the night.

We drove out to the coffee shop on the highway, and took the table next to the door. You know what Dear Reader? Some of this stuff I haven't thought about in years and I am seriously amazed that given a minimum of effort some of these memories come back clear as a bell.

We sat at that table and we talked. I found out so much about her and the more I learned the more I wanted to know. I don't think she knew it then but she had me completely ensnared, enamoured and enraptured.

It wasn't until we noticed that the sun was completely up that the spell was broken. The realization that I was going to have to drive her home prompted me to quickly invite her to breakfast. She agreed and I had her to myself for a few hours more.

Once the excuses and breakfast were done, I found myself dropping her off at her door. Before she could go in I blurted out that I had 2 tickets to a concert on Saturday night. Chantelle said "I would love to go with you pick me up at 7".

Oh shit, damn, what the hell was I going to do? I had just asked this gorgeous woman on a date and I had a girlfriend. Fuck, I felt sick to my stomach. Did this count as cheating? Oh my god, what the hell would my dad think? What was I going to do?

I couldn't sleep when I got home. I was invigorated from my night with Chantelle and excited by the prospect of seeing her again, at the same time disgusted with myself and unable to figure out what I was going to do about Jada. Completely unable to make a decision and with the clock rapidly approaching noon, I decided to drive over to Jada's house.

I pulled into the driveway and I just sat there. Jada must have seen me because within a few minutes she came out to the car. It must have been written all over my face, throughout my life I have often been accused of wearing my heart on my sleeve. Jada quickly asked me what was wrong.

This next part I am going to chalk up to my youth and inexperience. Only to ease my own conscious I told Jada that I couldn't see her anymore as I had met someone I wanted to get to know better and I couldn't do that and be with Jada. Just straight like that no sugar coating stupid eh? For not the first time in my life I watched a heart break only this time as I watched the pain creep into her face and the light go out in her eyes, I knew that I was the cause. Quietly Jada said "ok" and got out of the car. I watched her walk slowly into the drive and into the house.

As I backed out of her driveway I promised myself I would never hurt someone like that again. We never intend to do we. I felt like such a heel, a real asshole. I knew in my core though that I had made the right decision and I was free to get to know Chantelle.

Saturday came quickly and as Chantelle answered the door I saw the little black dress had been replaced by the little red dress, my heart did a full back flip (yes really my heart, don't be a pig Dear Reader).

The concert was good what I remember of it anyways. What I do clearly remember is the way she smiled all night long and when she asked me to dance how I had to stand far enough away, so my arousal wouldn't be too obvious. A task her dancing did little to ease for me.

Since I had had such a great time as I was driving her home I was struggling with a way to get to see her again. Before I knew it we were parked in front of her building. I didn't want to push my luck by asking her to coffee again so I managed to stammer out something like "I'll call you tomorrow" or something as equally poorly planned out. Her brilliant reply was "Aren't you going to walk me to my door?" As I am writing this I have a bit of a smile on my face, I wish you could see it. As I start remembering these things it seems that these girls all knew before I did exactly what was going to happen well before I did.

I was slightly embarrassed that I hadn't walked her to her door the previous weekend, so I hurried around to help her out of the car and to open the door for her. I walked her arm in mine right up to her apartment door.

She put her key in the lock and placed her finger on her lips (which for the record just brought attention to them) "Shhhh my babysitter is sleeping." I haven't really mentioned Shay-Lynne up to this point or barely at least, suffice to say Chantelle had a 2 and a bit year old, also she had a really crazy ex who would add excitement to our future endeavours. "Ok, I should be going then" I whispered as Chantelle pulled me into her apartment and pressed her lips to mine.

Since I was caught completely off guard it took a second for me to catch my breath and kiss her back. When I did I kissed her with a fervour and a passion I had yet to experience. It stood on its own, a kiss so different from the knowing kisses that Tanya and I had shared or the almost chaste kisses that Jada and I had exchanged. It was a hungry kiss, a questing kiss, a wanting kiss. It was exactly what it was supposed to be.

Amongst the scattered shoes and flung coats in Chantelle's entrance way, we shared a first kiss. It may not have been one of those first kisses for the ages but I would be lying if I told you that it wasn't a first kiss to be remembered.

Chantelle broke our kiss with a "whoa" and a little laugh. With a young mans ardour I hungrily groped for another kiss. She placed a finger on my lips and whispered "she is asleep come back tonight after Shay-Lynne is in bed." She gave me a quick peck and opened the door behind me. Understanding that this was my cue to leave, I quickly and quietly left.

I spent all day in a peculiar state of anticipation and disbelief. What was going to happen? Would I show up at Chantelle's only to have her say "oh, ya sorry, just kidding" with a look of disappointment on her face? I couldn't figure out why such an engaging woman wanted me, as I racked my brain I wasn't sure what it was that I had to offer her. Not being one to look a gift horse in the mouth as night neared I prepared to look my best........be prepared, have I mentioned I was a boy scout.

# 44

This tendency towards preparedness has served me well and as the zombies were tearing down civilization around me I knew what I needed to gather up and even had most of it conveniently located in the garage next to my truck, in case of just this emergency. I told you we planned for this exact occurrence. We had an emergency preparedness kit for power outages, floods, storms etc...also conveniently this served the dual purpose of a zombie survival kit. It only made sense to store such a kit in the garage.

The plan called for us to meet over at Sebastian's house. Coolers full of food, a couple of cases of bottled water, basic first aid supplies, a hand crank radio and all my hunting and camping gear was what I loaded into the truck.

Standing in my living room, dog by my side mostly ready to go. I was searching for some news, some direction from those in charge as I watched chaos expand its hold on man. Flipping through each channel, finding more than half of them off the air or broadcasting that singular tone, that steady beeping that 50 years earlier would have caused children all over North America to seek shelter underneath their school desks. Like that would have protected anyone from a nuclear holocaust. I stood, my flipping interrupted by an old episode of Gilligan's Island, its laugh track breaking my thoughts as I gathered my courage to leave.

A few more channel flicks and my favourite movie, "Are all men from the future such loud mouth braggarts" assaults me from my surround sound system and I can't help but mouth "nope just me baby." I know the dialogue so well that I can recite this movie word for word. The simple act of doing this transports me back in time. Was it merely months ago? I knew I loved her that night. I was still wrestling with the idea, I knew however deep in my heart. I had already fallen.

She was coming again to watch a movie, not any movie but the movie, my favourite movie, I was so excited. I even attempted to tidy up my place. Tonight I would share this movie with her. I also knew she probably wouldn't really like the movie. It was almost a rite of passage though. How could I love someone who hadn't seen it? Who wouldn't roll their eyes when I said "Give me some sugar baby" or

"Hello Mr. Fancypants"? How could I love someone who couldn't give me an "I pity you" smile when I randomly said "good, bad, I'm the guy with the gun"?

I remember how she laid her head on my shoulder. How I couldn't control myself and I would start reciting the movie. Almost instantly her hand would be over top of my mouth and she would nestle in even closer. I held her and we watched my favourite movie. A more perfect night I have never had.

I am sorry Dear Reader if my tears have obscured that last part? I miss her eh. It is the not knowing that is the hardest part. Will she make her way to me? Will I hold her in my arms again? I doubt it, I don't know. I do know that I will be here waiting if this is where she decides she wants to be.

The stirring speech from the parapet breaks train of thought and helps me to gather up the courage I will need to head out to Sebastian's, even though I know that there will be no Henry the Red to save the day.

As I pulled out of my driveway I was thinking that this nightmare didn't really begin all that long ago. Order had given way so swiftly that in the back of my mind I couldn't help but think, could human civilization crumble and fall worldwide in a matter of hours? In a quarter of a day? Could it be instantaneous like the life ending impact of a huge celestial body? Are humans the new dinosaur? Could kingdoms and centuries of history be recklessly overrun without substantial resistance? If all

this could happen, how hard was it to take the next fore-
seeable step? The eradication of every single human being on the planet in as little as 24 hours. I only briefly
allowed that negative train of thought. I knew what I had
to do. I had to get to Sebastian's.

# 45

You know that I believe in fate Dear Reader. Not in the sense of 3 old hags, spinning, measuring and cutting out the lengths of our lives. Fate in terms of predestination, I believe only the things that are supposed to happen to us are the things that happen. Fate however can only take us so far and it is what we do with the opportunities fate gives to us that take us that extra mile.

With that in mind let us go back in time to that Sunday, the Sunday after the Saturday, with the unknown before me I hesitantly knocked on Chantelle's door. She opened the door with a beaming smile that dispelled my doubts and had an infectiousness to it. This caused my own smile to creep onto my face. Just so you know I am not really the broad smiling type. I am more aptly described as brooding or introverted. I don't actually care for people all that much in general. I am however fiercely loyal to those I care about. In that moment though I wasn't pretending immediately fogged up my brain and I knew that I would let myself go. I knew when her smile hit me that the woman before me, this beautiful woman before me well, I was going to give her my heart.

We may have talked for a bit, I am sure we did. It was late and I don't remember what it was that we talked about.

What I do remember was that she had her back to me as she stood facing her balcony behind her couch. I walked over and tentatively put my hands on her shoulders. She stiffened slightly but allowed me to turn her so she was facing me. This time when we kissed, it was clouded with what was to come. This kiss was timid and testing. I would guess we were both afraid of the promise that this kiss held.

These tender, timid, testing kisses eventually gave way, their fortifications groaned as the tempest of passion swirled and roiled beneath them. Our defences shuddered under the assault of groping hands and the great walls tumbled with our clothing into a pile on the floor at our feet. It was an all consuming passion, a frenzied heat.

Watching us make love would have been a little like watching those old test videos from Los Alamos. The slowly expanding mushroom cloud, growing up and out until it blots out the sun.........and......BAM!!!! Unleashed, the buildings blow over, mannequins burst apart, hells fury unleashed, Chantelle collapsing into my arms, sweat dripping from our bodies. The couch cracking and collapsing beneath us.

Have you ever been in a passion based relationship Dear Reader? They burn so hot from the cornerstone up. A tempest and an inferno. They burn fast, they burn hot, but eventually they will burn out. When you use your memory to sift through the remaining ashes, you will find the stories that make you blush and those that make you laugh. The bits and pieces of real and imagined romance that helped to shape the person you are. You know what I mean Dear Reader, don't you?

That half remembered picnic in the field behind your house. The bouquet of flowers or was it a stuffed bear? Maybe you wrote her or him a poem? Maybe I did too? I can't clearly remember the ash clouds the water. In some ways though I must have tried.

More clearly I can remember the hurried rush out the door clothes in hand, wearing only boxers attempting to sneak down the fire escape when the crazy violent ex just showed up at her building. The unenviable decision of do I put on clothes or untie her from the bed when my mother pounded on the door at 3 in the morning. I will leave it to your imagination Dear Reader which choice I made. Most embarrassing of all was borrowing mom and dad's car to go out on a Saturday night, and getting yelled at on Sunday morning on our way to church, because we must have left the window open and "the seat is wet". Ha ha ha I can't help but smile as I remember. I had never seen Chantelle turn such a shade of scarlet red before.

Being with and loving Chantelle taught me a very important life lesson. This lesson being that my heart and sex are intertwined. If I give the latter, the former will follow. I know that it is dangerous to judge my insides by other people's outsides; it has however been my experience that most other guys aren't wired this way. So I learned from Chantelle to be careful who I sleep with because my heart will inevitably follow.

This last time I gave my heart first. I know you are forming a picture of that tale as bits and pieces leach in here and there. Mostly this is happening because she is on my mind. Even as I reminisce about past loves both good and bad, I can't help but think of her. The emptiness I feel without her is prevailing.

Though what Chantelle and I had was hot. We had different ideas on the direction that our relationship should take. I loved her and I wanted to marry her and help raise Shay. It was a very disconcerting experience when years later, while talking on face book to reconcile the woman she was becoming, with the little girl that had ridden on my shoulders or that I had thrown across the room into a pile of stuffed toys when she jumped on my head excitedly to wake me up because she wanted someone to play with. I am sure Mark Brankin would get a kick out of the fact that during this time I became quite adept at playing with my little horseys. Here she was talking about boys and other nefarious subjects.

At that time in her life Chantelle was what I would later come to recognize as a bit of a party girl. At that time in her life drinking partying and other things took priority over what I had to offer her. To be fair she never led me down a garden path and I doubt there were many others. I have however felt that I didn't need to scratch the surface too deeply to find things that would further wound my heart.

It took a long time to learn the lessons that I needed to from Chantelle and I behaved in a reprehensible manner as well. One time after we were done, there was an opportunity for us to reconcile. Just to hurt her, I used her at the bar I worked at then took off to spend the night at some stripper's house. I didn't sleep with the dancer I just wanted to hurt Chantelle. One of my worst moments for sure.

I know.....I can almost hear your screams of protest Dear Reader yet again. WAIT A MINUTE!!!! HOLD UP!!! WHAT THE FUCK!!! I am sure the last thing you were expecting was such poor behaviour and the appearance of a stripper in a story involving a woman I claim to love. Look.......at no point in this narrative have I claimed to be perfect. So try your best not to judge. I have made more mistakes when it comes to love than I can even remember. I have hurt people who didn't deserve it and a few who did. I have cried myself to sleep and felt true joy. Love is crazy and so am I. This last time is the closest to right I have ever had it, we didn't jump into bed together we let things grow slow and yet she's not here so, well who knows right. Please just try not to judge, especially the stripper's part. Some of the best friends I have ever had have been dancers. These constant interruptions where I feel like I must explain myself are becoming tiresome. A dancer is just a person trying to do a job. It requires a thick skin and a high level of athleticism, also commitment if you want to be good at what you do. So lay off dancers!..... besides..... never mind we will get there if that is where this story takes us.

# 46

We stood like this many nights. My arm around her shoulders staring up at the sky overhead. With each falling star a variation of the same wish, may this moment last forever. Getting to know each other through hushed whispers. We would make our way to where we could sit down.

"You should sit down here, preferably like you aren't afraid of me."

"Don't be stupid Greg; I'm not afraid of you."

"Then come here then." I said as I nudged her in. she would curl up against me and after a moment I could feel her relax against my body. I gently lay my hand on the side of her face, softly running a finger along her ear; she pressed the other against the drumbeat of my heart. I touched a light kiss to her forehead.

Then another and another on her cheek. She tilts her face to me, and without hesitation, I accept the invitation and find her lips. Gently, open-mouthed I slanted my lips across hers and slid my fingers into her hair. She kissed me back, her mouth opening and her hands climbing up to my shoulders and neck. Soon she pulls me down and we sink together to the ground.

A sound, I hear it first and went stiff, I try to pull away "stop, stop" I whisper. A flame sparks in the quiet darkness, he is having a smoke. We sit up quietly. I study the guarded way that she sits there, the dark shutter of her lashes. I realize that she has spent a lifetime building walls to protect herself, since no one else did. The closing door signals that we are alone again.

"I want to take care of you."

"Fuck I don't need yo_____"

My lips cut her off, as I cup her face and bring her forward. The flush in her cheeks burns my palms, her breath catching in her throat. I pushed past the moment of uncertainty and surprise, roaming and tasting and playing on her lips until they fell open on a sigh. I deepened the kiss, the age old heat of young love simmering with wisdom and time, boiling into a wild and unmet need to have her. She leans into me, hands gripping my shirt and breasts pressing my chest. We kissed and stroked and shared one another's breath while the world faded to nothing. I pressed her close and held her tight. Only when she ground her hips into me did we stop. "Wait, wait" it is too much, it is too fast. I want this to be different; I want her to know how much I love her first. I want it to be as special as she has become to me. She has saved my life. I want to change her's. Reality....I sit here alone by my fire. Oh the gods do jest. She knows I love her what more can I ask.

# 47

They came for me last evening. I am not sure what alerted them, whether the light of my campfire that I write by or maybe the smell of meat cooking over that same open flame. Either way they must have been watching me for a while trying to determine when I would be most vulnerable.

The shower, how stupid of me to not be prepared. When I set up the shower I guess in my excitement at the idea of hot water I never considered how vulnerable showering would leave me. Ingeniously I placed an old black plastic tank up high in a tree and filled it with water. The sun heats the water all day and as twilight begins to fall, glory of glories, hot water to scrub myself clean with.

You know what I am talking about you survived. In fact I would guess that you Dear Reader have set down these pages to go see if the apparatus is still there so you can fill it up and go have a shower yourself. Since I have probably lost you for a bit I guess it is safe to write whatever I want. Just in case you have decided to stay with me, I am going to take the opportunity to thank you once again for staying with me this far. It helps me to imagine you here as I tell my tale and I appreciate the company.

Dear Reader we are rounding the bend together the finish is almost in sight. Let me ask you, were you a NASCAR fan BZE? I never really understood the appeal. Imagine the announcers "wasn't that an exciting left turn Bob!" ha ha ha. I can almost see from here the end of the tale that I have to tell. So if you hold on Dear Reader we will get there together, provided of course that we both survive.

So as I started saying "they came for me last night" in the shower. Before you get all flustered asking whether or not I have been bitten, and you start worrying that I won't be able to continue this tale after you have invested your time into it. Relax. Those who came last night were men.

The collapse of civilization has peeled back the veneer of civility. While not only leaving us with the abominations of the walking dead to deal with, also created a monster more heinous than even the most terrifying horror movies could have hinted at. A Desperate Man. Take away all the rules, add a dash of fear, a pinch of cowardice and you have a recipe for a monster of epic proportions. A thing to haunt the dreams of Freddy, Jason and Pinhead, a desperate man.

There were 4 of them. I could condemn them for their cowardice, if I didn't understand it. If I didn't pity them. They don't have the light of love to guide them. So there I stood naked, glorying in the heat and freshness, as the water ran down my body.

Was it the sensation of being watched or the half heard sound of a twig snapping? I can't rightly recall. My muscles tensed and I ducked just in time to save my life. Half blind with soap in my eyes I swung in the direction that I felt the attack had come from. Though it had been years I felt the familiar yet unique sensation of a fist connecting with flesh. I felt my knuckles compress and groan as I felt my assailants jaw give way and unhinge. A second set of fists connects with my ribs. The wind rushing out of me as I felt ribs snap and crack. Lashing out with my elbow I can feel a collar bone break, as an uppercut breaks my nose. I feel my fingers and knuckles breaking as my fists connect. A metal bar connects with my head and the last thing I see is my spattered blood as I deflate and their feet start to connect with my head. The world goes black to a soundtrack of their feral laughter.

I really don't know if it was hours or days before I reluctantly swam back to reality. I slowly drifted from the darkness to the light in increments of pain, until I opened my eyes to excruciating brilliance. My face was encrusted with snot and tears, blood rivulets dried on my body. A map to my pain. Hot spots a deep purple hold the promise of a body painted in rainbow colours.

Minutes or hours pass. An inventory of my meagre belongings shows less.

We, Dear Reader sit and talk of days gone by. A life lived and lost, of loves loved and not forgotten but gone nonetheless. Up until now we may have shared some laughs as I have bared my soul to you. Today my body is broken, but my heart beats on. So I will continue this journey. Though I can feel my sanity slipping, I will wait. It is what I told her I would do.

Moving on from here and now that you know Chantelle's role in this tale. Let us go back to a young man recovering with a cast on his leg from hip to ankle with a little window cut out so the dressing could be changed.

# 48

$I$ was lying in my room, staring at the ceiling and completely bored out of my mind. I made the decision that I wanted to go back to work. I am stubborn eh? Against almost everyone's advice with my cane in hand I went back on what we called light duty. If you know anything about the hunting, fishing tourism industry you know that there is really no such thing.

I am sorry Dear Reader as I look over the last few lines; it seems as if all the heart has gone out of my tale. Maybe it is the fact that each breath reminds me of how a broken rib feels, 5 times over. My nose and cheek are broken and to top it off I found some grey hairs in my beard.

I guess it is only fitting to write about such a dark time while going through a dark time. See, I went back to work not out of some sense of misguided nobleness, though I would like to tell it that way. The time to shine things up has long past. From here on how about we just tell it like it was, warts and all.

I was lying in my room and I had no idea what I was going to do with the rest of my life. College had pulled my acceptance; there was no way that I could have passed the physical to be a paramedic with my "bum" knee. With no real prospects and no real hope, I decided to go back to work. This part of the story just doesn't seem to want to come out. Let us leave it for a bit. Let's move on and flow with the muse.

The door to Sebastian's house was open. Given the circumstances I didn't feel it was necessary for me to knock or ring the bell. I nudged the door open with my foot. It swung wide and I took a moment to study the entrance way. I had been here lots since Sebastian bought it but now the familiar seemed strange, nothing quite in its proper place.

The first floor showed much evidence of Sebastian's long standing habits, comfortable furniture well used a clearly defined napping print in the couch cushions. A Clive Barker book was half open on the end table. Sebastian's doll collection.....pardon me....action figure collection, each in its place.

I quietly approached the stairs to the second floor. I climbed the stairs, keeping my back to the wall so I could see both the top and the bottom of the stairs.

The solid wood door to the master bedroom had been completely ripped off of its hinges. Cracked almost in half it lay on the floor in the hallway. The hinges had been bent in the frame by the force that had ripped away the door.

If Sebastian had sought safety here it had not lasted long. Expecting a slaughterhouse or an outrage so inhumane that it could not be anticipated, I hesitated to enter the bedroom.

When I walked in however I saw no signs of violence. No one was in the walk in closet. When I tried the master baths door I found it was locked.

Leaning against the door I whispered "Sebastian? Sebastian are you there?" if he answered me it was too quiet for me to hear. "Seb, it's me Greg, you in there? Are you alright?" When I received no answer, I stepped back from the door and kicked it hard.

It took me 3 kicks to open the door. I looked in and recoiled, I turned away in visceral horror and revulsion.

Eyeless his head hollowed out as completely as a Halloween pumpkin. Sebastian sat on the floor resting against the side of the bathtub. Between his knees was the short barrelled, pump action shotgun that he had sucked on.

I instinctively knew that he had retreated to the bathroom and blew his brains out to avoid coming face to face with whatever tore down the bedroom door. I suppose when the shotgun was heard, they must have known what he had done and had no further interest in him.

I can't really say as I blame him. This new reality, the things we need to face to survive, watching all that man has built crumble and fall. I have felt at times that it would be easier to punch my own ticket. I have survived thus far though. Wouldn't that be a shock Dear Reader you have read up to this point and……..

Nothing, no more story. As far as practical jokes go I think that would be in poor taste. I will finish my tale, that much I can promise you. Back to it I guess?

So despite the advice of just about everyone in my life, cast on my leg, cane in hand, I returned to work on "light duty".

I could write about the forest fire we had to fight, how we even had to draft the guests to save the camp. All you really need to know is that it was a bad idea to go back to work so early. Turns out that I was now afraid of boats.

I told you so or more accurately, I thought so is probably going through your head Dear Reader.

Eleven days after returning to work a bad storm blew in. it was camp policy to move the boats across the lake to a sheltered bay during storms. Taking my boat across the waves were crashing against the boat tossing us to and fro. Reminiscent of my accident, I became gripped with panic. Totally paralyzed with fear, and with great shame I had to be rescued. When I was brought to the beach, head down I limped up to my quarters. Alone I started to pack up my gear. Tough decision for the boss, I understood it though. You couldn't have a fishing guide on staff who might freeze or panic with guests in the boat. He gave me all the money that was outstanding and he drove me to my parent's house.

I had to break in because no one was home. My mood got darker and darker as I sat in my basement contemplating my future or lack there of. The neat little package I had created for my life had just burst wide open. I wasn't sure if I had it in me to pick up the pieces.

I took my parents car down to the liquor store and I bought a bottle of my favourite scotch. I returned home and poured myself a stiff glass intending to escape for a bit. 8 days later I sobered up in Winnipeg 400 km away.

# 49

*I* had a job when I sobered up, so I stayed. Really it was as simple as that. That 8 day period of my life is gone forever. The job I had was at the Maryland Hotel. That cast of characters and that time in my life really deserves a book in its own right.

It seems fitting that I write about the Maryland with a broken face and broken ribs. It was there that I really learned to take the boyish schoolyard brawl to the next level.

"YOU FUCK!! It's because I'm an Indian isn't it! I bet if I was a blonde with big tits you would do it!!"

"No sir" I stammer "I just don't have change for an American 100 dollar bill.

"FUCK YOU, You FUCKIN WHITEY!!!!"

"Look sir in the past 30 seconds you have called me a racist and sexist, please understand that I can't do it." I attempted to placate him using a soothing tone.

There was more yelling and I lose my patience. I pressed the button to alert security. As I did that I leapt over the front desk, at the same time grabbing him by the hair and driving him face first into the counter top. Kalifornia arrives and adds his boots to mine until a thin red stream begins to leak from his ear. Then we pick him up and throw him out into the parking lot.

I hum and tap my foot to the music pounding in from the bar as I mop up the blood and bits of teeth. 2 hours done, 6 to go. An average day, an average shift, all in a days work at the Maryland Hotel.

Often in the years that followed if we were able to connect and reminisce we would talk about how outrageous and unbelievable our years at the Maryland really were. Unless you lived it, there was no way you could ever really understand. It really was refined insanity.

It was 2 years where a punch was thrown every shift. A level of violence that was so extreme, someone fought for their life every night.

This severe and intense setting was only interrupted by a beauty in a green velvet dress. It all seems kind of silly looking back now but I loved Christine deeply at the time. I was dumbstruck when she walked by, my mouth agape barely able to mumble "who is that?"

As I think about how beautiful Christine looked that night the memory shimmers and shifts. I see her standing up in the bow of the boat, fishing rod in hand and she is framed by the setting sun. I wish I had the words to portray to you Dear Reader with some level of accuracy how truly beautiful she was, is, I hope.

I find it strange as we have been heading to this point; I really felt I would have more to say about Christine and The Maryland. I don't, possibly because as I have said that time at the Maryland is worthy of a book all its own. How could I really do it justice by summing it up in a few words here? I will try though, I have to really. That time was too important in refining the man I would become to leave out. It would not be fair to you Dear Reader. I might as well just say I fell in love and so I wait.

## The End

I know, I know that is cheap and I won't do it instead let me introduce to you this cast of characters, that called ourselves the Maryland Mafia. I will do my best to disguise identities to protect the guilty, of which there are quite a few and the innocent as well just in case there is someone who is. Let us Dear Reader get to know them now.

# 50

The thunderous thumping of the dance music abruptly changes. The wailing guitar interrupts whatever I was I was doing. This song was a signal to those of us scattered throughout the bar. Trouble. I see the mob forming near the door as the fight spills out into the parking lot.

Nigel the DJ was at the back of the crowd frantically waving us over. Briefly earlier we have already met Nigel, if you remember Nigel took his role of wingman very seriously. Nigel was about 5'6" tall and had a lazy eye. Now Nigel was quite the ladies man and at last count had about 14 kids. The running joke amongst us was, all Nigel had to do was look at a girl the wrong way and she would miss her period. Get it, ha ha ha, he had a lazy eye. Ok forget it you had to be there. Despite his short stature you could always find Nigel in the middle of whatever brawl was currently happening, you knew he had your back. Even if it was just to yell "Hey dude! Your back just got hit twice!"

One of the fondest memories I have of Nigel is of a camping trip that we took together, with Kalifornia and his future wife. Nigel was a city boy in every sense of the word. We put him in the bow of the boat to watch for rocks on our trip out to the island we were going to be camping on. Since it was night we gave him a flashlight and to him to keep his eye peeled (ha-ha). His terror at the prospect of "rocks" was only matched by the knowledge we gave him after a handful of magic mushrooms that bears could swim.

The mob moves slowly as I elbow my way through. I feel like I am trying to swim in molasses. I see Kalifornia out of the corner of my eye as he hits a guy so hard that his glasses fly off his face and shatter against the far wall.

Kalifornia was the nominal leader of our "crew". It was he who coined the phrase "Maryland Mafia" and he was the epitome of the slick ladies man. If he was an x man his uncanny ability would be to attract phone numbers. I can remember one time he took 3 dancers upstairs and eventually when he returned his white t-shirt was soaked through with red bloody claw marks.

I see his hair flying about as wildly as his fists as he tries to quell what is rapidly becoming a riot.

Hippie picks up a guy and tosses him like a rag doll through some poor cars windshield. Hippie stands out because he is so big. No other word really could do him justice he was big. At 6'8" and just over 300 pounds, he truly was a beast. Legend had it that he was born with a full head of hair so hence the nickname, Hippie. To give you a taste of his power once at Silverado's he snuck up behind me and picked me up and tossed at least 5 feet over his head. At this time I was a bout 225 pounds.

I see Scott dragging himself back into the club, the handle of a hatchet embedded into his shoulder. "Oh shit this is getting serious" I think to my self as a short bladed knife grazes my shoulder blade. I grab a head and smash it into the brick wall.

The hammer brothers are fighting back to back now. These boys made sure that we never ran out of whatever it was that we felt we needed to add to the party. Two tanks kicking and punching their way through our parking lot. The older is kicking some poor schmucks head off of the curb while the younger in a flurry of fists is holding off 3 guys. Grabbing one of them by the throat and hurling him 10 yards.

Hill stands alone at the far end of the parking lot. In between the ashtray being broken on my chin and the next duck. I see him running a guy along a chain link fence like it was a cheese grater.

"Oh my god!" I can't help but exclaim as big Christine (not my Christine but another bouncer hence the big before her name) takes a baseball bat to the mouth. Without missing a beat she spits out her teeth and continues to feed punches to the guy she has in a head lock. She is the toughest woman I have ever met.

Darcy and Darcy fight back to back a flurry of punches and kicks. The larger unhooks the bear spray and adds a cloud to every face he doesn't recognize including a visiting friend of mine. The rioting crowd grips its face and cries out from the burning.

A peripheral cast of cocktail waitresses, bartenders, strippers and hangers on round out the cast in the parking lot.

40 minutes and things have calmed down; we have tended to our wounds and are back doing what it is we do. We lived at that time by the 3 F's we were either Fighting, Fucking, or Falling down drunk. We were boisterous and if we decided we were all going out that night the chance were better than average that we were getting barred from yet another club. It was an exciting and intense time in my life.

It was at this time, that my dad was diagnosed with cancer.

# 51

My lips gently caress her cheek, as my hand softly brushes away her hair. Her eyelids flicker and flutter hinting and teasing at the soft beauty hidden behind.

"Good morning beautiful" I quietly whisper.

"Mmmm, good morning" she says as she stretches and wraps her arms around me, pulling me down to her. Her lips just touch mine and the sharp exquisite current rushes to my toes.

I whisper again "hey pretty lady".

A satisfied groan, as she snuggles in close to me.

"I love you" was what I wanted to say. Instead I say "it is time, let's go".

She grips me tighter "not yet".

The soft lapping of the waves against the beach awakens me. As this work progresses Dear Reader the emptiness gets easier to deal with. The dreams hurt though; remembering is like picking at a festering wound. At least my sleep is not haunted by the horrors I have seen on the way here. I miss the dog too he was an innocent.

Enough procrastinating. I suppose it doesn't come as a big shock to you, I have either hinted at or outright told you my dad got cancer. I don't really feel like flipping back to find out which it was.

The news just floored me. My parents told me over the phone and I had never not once until that moment even considered the idea that my dad might die.

As you have read my tale thus far you know that I was no stranger to death Dear Reader. I understood the process. I had even for my young age confronted my own mortality a time or two.

The thought of my dad dying though had never not once ever even crossed my mind.

Now, not only did it cross my mind but it settled into my heart. I realized all at once that my dad could and would one day die. Probably sooner rather than later. Holy shit eh? In a matter of seconds 24 years of memories tumbled through my head, racing each other to reach my consciousness.

It is kind of funny you know, with all the things that my dad was apart of in my life whenever I start to think of him I think of fishing. It's not that we spent a lot of time fishing. I guess it's just that we spent some of our best times fishing. It was one of those times for us when we really got to talk. Often these conversations would end with him saying "Geez, don't tell your mother that".

We were floating in a hidden bay that was one of my northern hotspots on Eagle Lake. I wonder if I can successfully describe the day to you Dear Reader. If you would indulge me please.

The heat of the day was amplified by the aluminum of the boat. The sun was beating down on us relentlessly. The whir of the spinning reel the only sound until the daredevil spoon hits the water. The strike, the fight, rod bending, working her back and forth, drag set just right. Dad grabs the net and helps me land the 5 pound jackfish.

"You are cleaning that slimy thing, or throw her back" says dad.

"Look dad, if I fry it up I defy you to tell me the difference" I reply. I add the fish to my rapidly filling stringer.

I comment "hey old man your stringer is looking a little light".

As if in response dad sets his hook "get the net son, let me show you how it's done". A couple of minute's later dad holds up proudly his 3 pound walleye "you were saying boy?"

Conceding the point "nice fish" I say.

Not wanting to be outdone, I switch to a chartreuse jig head with a minnow and I settle into the boat seat, kicking my feet up on the gunnels.

Soaking in the sun, lazily I asked "Hey dad how did you make it work with mom?"

"I do what I say I'm going to do, I try to love her more each day than the day before and I don't mind sitting on benches in malls for hours while your mom shops, I love your mother."

I slowly sucked my cigarette contemplating his words. Life with my father was a lot like that. He was a man of few words. When he did tell you something you could tell that the words were weighed and measured, they usually required you to think them through.

# 52

ap, tap, tap. Such an innocent sound, imagine a maestro preparing his orchestra. Tap, tap, tap. The sound that haunts my dreams. That simple tapping broke the spell you see, it shattered the illusion, ended the dream, and broke the spell.

Tap, tap, tap, who would have guessed it eh?

Peering into it'd depths like a proverbial soothsayer hunched over his crystal ball; I held the ring in my hands. Its single stone revealed and hinted at my future. Within it's depths I saw her smile, within its depths her eyes held me.

Whether for the first time or the hundredth time when I gazed deep into it I heard her say yes; and I felt complete. The fantasy slowly coalesced around me. It was so easy for me to lose myself in a world of our laughter and stolen kisses. So easy to see and feel the dream. I can feel the way her soft body moulded to mine, the way she felt against me. I feel whole.

Tap, tap, tap. A lone finger dragging against the window. A shambling hulking corpse dragging his was along my truck. Lost in my mind I lost sight of the danger. He is only the vanguard, and the horde begins to swarm around me. Their low moans reverberating through the truck windows. I am trapped, I am done for. The pup's hackles raise and his low growling lends a back beat to moaning outside.

Panic grips me, did they or was it I smash the glass. I can feel myself being ripped from the truck. Thick clothing protecting me from the gnashing teeth. I yell for the dog only to see him wrenched from the vehicle. Torn asunder his gore splats my face. Maybe he is the lucky one torn to pieces not even enough left to reanimate. Spared a fate worse than death.

Once weeks later I saw a reanimated dog so overcome with its desire to consume flesh that it was tearing off rotting chunks from it's own haunches and eating them. The horde drove me off; it wasn't safe to wait there anymore. I moved on to here the backup. So now I wait.

# 53

*I* grab her from behind, my deep voice resonating and vibrating all through her as I press my chest to her back "est-ce que aime une danse privee"? I whispered this in her ear.

"Mmmm" she groans against me as she smiles. I lovingly kiss her neck, tiny kisses climbing their way up to her ear lobe......I bite softly.

I grasp her hand, twirl her once around the kitchen and then I pull her in tight against me. Looking, gazing into her deeply pooling hazel eyes I half growl and half whisper "je t'aime ma belle femme, je pense, je suis une romantique au couer."

"Fuck Greg, speak English or kis...." No chance to finish as I gently press my lips to hers.

I kiss her hungrily, tasting our passion, drawing her closer. With my lips pressed to hers I begin to dance us around the kitchen. At first she resists the dancing, our hungry kisses convince her to stay in my arms. The song in my head over I dip her once "I love you" was all that I could say. It was all that she could hear and she smiled. In her eyes I saw how easy it would be for me to fall and I knew that that is just what I would do each time I looked into her eyes.

"How about we make some butter tarts?"

The loud pop of a pine knot deep within the fire interrupts my daydreaming. I once again become aware of the pain in my ribs and a hurt that runs so much deeper.

Damn my mind!!! When is it going to be enough this waiting this not knowing! Must I be tormented in my sleep as well! It is enough to make you want to scream, I love her! Isn't that enough? There is no answer I don't expect one. Loving her means I have to hope she is happy, wherever she is.

I apologize Dear Reader for my outburst; I do appreciate your company. Maybe this isolation is finally getting to me but I can almost picture you here next to me. I guess as I write I imagine you here, this is probably the first step into madness though. Oh well even madness might provide some blessed relief.

Procrastination has always been a strong suit of mine but I guess it is time. Let me tell you about a snowstorm.

It was whiteout conditions, maddeningly so as I tried to navigate the 401 highway. Was it the snow or the tears threatening to burst at any moment that made driving so treacherous?

Mom had called an hour ago and told me it was time to make the drive to London. It was difficult to drive, you try and drive while memories burst forth and roar through your mind.

A piggyback ride, a book read, waving me home from third base, cheering, patient, kind, soft and hard. My dad, my coach, my Sunday school teacher, my confidant, my friend. A swirling tempest, chaotically churning, consuming my mind and threatening my heart.

4 years had come and gone in the blink of an eye, now the day was here, I was going to lose my father. Even as I write this here and now Dear Reader, I realize how much I still miss him. The snow caused me to have to pull over for a few hours and I couldn't nap, I couldn't shut off my head.

When we arrived finally, I burst into the hospital room; I was terrified that I would be too late and remembering Uncle Larry.

"Easy kiddo, catch your breath" dad says to me.

"Oh shit old man, you had me scared that I was a day late and a dollar short" I said relief filling my voice.

"Not yet, not yet" was all he said.

I couldn't control my emotions anymore as I apologized to him for my blubbering and boohooing like a cry-baby.

"It's ok Greg we knew this day was coming" leave it to dad to try and provide me with comfort while he was dying.

"I know dad, I know but how can we ever be prepared?" I questioned him.

"Trust in the plan." Was his answer.

I talked everyday with dad on the phone, I wasn't sure how to live life without his love guidance and counsel.

I could take the time here to write out the bulk of our bedside conversations. I will sum it up though, a lot of tears and suffice to say it was an opportunity for both of us to say the things we needed to say to each other. For my father to impart some last minute advice and for me to assure him that I would be ok.

At one point, he was a tough bugger and managed to hold on for almost 2 more weeks, I decided that as a treat for him I would make him some butter tarts.

My mothers butter tarts were known far and wide as by far and away the best butter tarts ever. As I got older I had taken to making them for myself. After dropping them off, dad waved me over. By this time he was really weak and he didn't waste his energy. Expecting something profound I leaned in close so I could hear what he had to say. In a whispered voice he said "thanks for the butter tarts." He winked at me and pointed over to the bedside table. There sat a small jewellery box, as I picked it up he nodded. Inside the box was a small silver chain.

He smiled his smile. I you had ever seen it you would know what I am talking about. As I clasp the chain around my neck, I hugged him and cried as I told him how much I loved him.

The whole 2 weeks I stayed with dad and for the last 2 years of his life we talked every single day. We had plenty of time to say the things that needed to be said. I have peace knowing how we ended things.

How could I have predicted that the last words my dad would ever say to me were "thanks for the butter tarts"? I kept that silver chain around my neck and it protected me until the day I took it off.

Though dad wasn't talking anymore that didn't stop me from sitting with him and talking. Sharing stories, wild hunting trips, fish tales, life, love. Each night before I would go to sleep I would lean in and whisper "the best dad, my best friend, I love you dad". So I know what my last words to him were. If me and the old man were in competition I might add much better than "thanks for the butter tarts".

# 54

Alone last night I had a horrible thought. This rending of the soul may not be mine alone and I wept at the thought of her in pain. I don't want her to hurt. Does she struggle or has she given me up for lost. I hope she has moved passed it, given me up for lost. I hope she has a reason to smile. These thoughts tear at my soul. I wanted our life so badly; it was worth the sacrifice of my old life. She must not suffer. It is enough to make a man mad. Can you see me gnashing my teeth, pulling at my hair, screaming like a feral child "I LOVE YOU!!!" haggard and bedraggled what a sight I must have made?

Screaming and crying up to heaven like a primitive savage imploring his cruel and avarical gods for some boon. Sacrificing my tender hold on sanity, unable to hold it together, I break down.

Head in my hands, tears streaming down my face. Sitting on the toilet, I have no idea what to try next? I realize how hard it must have been for my dad. The overwhelming urge to call him for advice, overcome by the memory I can't. I don't know what to do about Jody. I can't reach him I am so worried, we don't know where he is. Though he infuriates me, mostly because he is like me at that age. Dad would know what to do of that I am sure. Unable to hold it all together I breakdown.

I can't help her. Whatever she goes through I am trapped and helpless. I just wish I could take her pain on. I hope she knows how much she is loved. She must know? How could she not? She need only look to the glittering silver chain that she wears about her neck. I sit exhausted by the fire, tired and worn, my tiny sobs a release.

# 55

Greg. Pssst! Greg, get up, Greg wake up! He is gone. Greg, Greg, your dad is dead. While I slept next to him my father died alone. Oh sure I was in the room, and before I laid down I told him how much I loved him, so at least I have that. For all intents and purposes though he was alone. He died without me holding his hand, to tell him a funny story so his mind could fill up with happy memories. Like the time we were fishing down at flat rock and in my 6 year old casting zeal I cast myself right into the lake. Dad had, had to jump in and fish me out. I could have told a thousand stories, rehashed a million memories, filled his head up with happiness as he left. I didn't do that for him, I slumbered. I am sure dad doesn't blame me though he died at 3 am.

I often wonder where dad went. Erin went home, where did dad choose to go? I would like to believe that if you had of been in the backyard of our house in Dryden you would have seen dad take one last walk through the garden he loved so much.

As you know by now Dear Reader I have had the misfortune a time or two of watching a heart break. That night through the phone, I heard a heart break. Such a sound can sorrow make. A noise that still haunts my dreams and waking hours. I heard the sound of a heart and soul being rendered as mom was told that dad had left us. It was horrible, it was awful, and it was the most pain I had ever felt up to that point. Soooo, I got married.

I am nearing the end of my tale now. It may seem to you Dear Reader that there is so much that I have left out and maybe that is the case. More than that though Dear Reader I have to save some memories just for me.

So ya a lot happened, I got married, I got separated, we had a bunch of foster kids, I did some good, I did some bad. Marriages fail all the time. I let mine. Times with my wife were good, better in fact than I felt I deserved. We were happy a lot. I wasn't happy enough. So I left. I wasn't sure what my future would hold, nonetheless I left.

With dad I should have known, I think I did, but I was surprised anyways. When someone you love dies you don't lose them all at once, you lose them one small piece at a time. Their scent slowly fades, and then their voice, you gather up the pieces and the memories hoping to stave off the inevitable. I wonder will it be the same when this love dies, will we let it.

I hesitate to go there but her words echo in my head, her lips were so close almost touching my ear, her breath tickles me "if you weren't married, it would be you taking me home tonight."

# 56

"If you weren't married it would be you taking me home tonight."

Those words haunt me as I sit alone listening to some country singer remind me that scarecrows and devils are the only thing that is out this late, and what that says about me is probably true". The scents of sex swirl and mix with the smell of booze as I wait for the light to change from crimson to emerald. I am satiated yet empty. The light changes and once again I am speeding to my destiny.

A future awaits me, a slow coalescing. I am starting to see, starting to know what I must do; wobbly and overcome I get out of my car.

As my key enters the lock, I faintly hear a poorly contained whine. I brace myself for the assault. I open the door and she leaps at me her excitement no longer containable.

A few small wet drops splatter on my boot as she try's to lick my face. I wrassle her down to the floor. Laughing out loud, we are playing now. Her playful nips lead to pats on her belly and scratches behind her ears. We roll on the ground together.

"Come on girl" I say and it is off to bed. She nuzzles in as close as she can and I begin to pet her belly.

My phone vibrates above my head. I don't need to be psychic to know who it is and what it says. "Please", "I miss you", "I want you", "come back", "again please".

As I reach for my phone I am overcome by the memories of a hundred nights and ten thousand kisses.

A hurried frenzied passion, an unassailable tempest. A hurricanned mess of clothing, a couch, a pool table, a bed, a bathtub, all rush past me. I see lips hungrily searching for succour, thrashing cries of passion, a sweet penetration, a bestial pounding.

We collapse together, sweating and panting. Satiated yet empty. I get dressed in the dark. I button my shirt to her soft drug induced snoring and I slip out the back door, while hoping her daughter doesn't wake up. Our dirty secret known.

As my hand touches my phone reality and daytime come crashing down around me. "Don't touch me", "I don't want a real relationship", "rub my back". The phone feels cold in my hands and so I set it down. It is too heavy for me to pick up anyways. How can I end this come here go away life? I cannot support its weight anymore. How can I escape the web my heart has spun....maybe Hugh's phone weighs less?

To my pups rhythmic breathing I eventually lose myself to sleep..... The wind rolls over me in waves. I have to lean into it to brace myself. I can only place one foot in front of the other. This tired trudging leads me one step closer, with each heavy step a rising sense of dread. It creeps, it crawls, grasping its way up my body, and it seeps into my soul. I try to look back so I can see what I am running from. My neck creaks and groans, frozen like rusted machine parts, it won't budge. I gaze downward at the barren rock strewn path in front of me. Loose rocks, exposed roots uneven footing are the pitfalls in front of me. I don't want to see anymore. My treacherous eyes, obeying an unseen puppeteer, slowly they are raised up. I will them to close. I imagine them as lead curtains; I will them to be heavier and heavier. Yet they betray me.

A lone ragged pine stands on top of the hill in front of me. Despairs sentinel.

Dangling from a lonely branch I can sense his freedom. I can't stop myself from gazing on his face. His tongue swollen and protruding, safe now it no longer wags, rumour and innuendo can now longer harm him. Eye's sightless and cloudy, the deep blue turned milky, no longer can he see the hurt. Swaying to the rhythm of the gently rolling breeze. I see the grey clouds rolling in and as I turn my face to the sky they burst drenching my face......I am thinking that Shakespeare said it best that "cowards die many times before their deaths; the valiant never taste of death but once. Of all the wonders that I yet have heard it seems to me most strange that men should fear, seeing that death, a necessary end, will come when it will come"...... I awaken.

Her tongue is lapping at my face.

"Alright, alright you horrid beast!" her excited whining tells me it is time to take her out for a pee.

# 57

So here we are Dear Reader, poised on the edge of my mind, the edge of a cliff, together we face the moment you have been waiting for. I know it is hard to believe that we are here already. Faced with the prospect of the hanged man behind us and the abyss of the unknown in front of us. What do we do Dear Reader? What do we do?

Peering over the edge our gaze is drawn, down, down, down. Blackness and wispy mist obscure whatever it is that we are looking for on the bottom. Our answers aren't there anyways. Going to the bottom will only have an outcome that we can easily predict. Just look to the hanged man and you will see how this story ends. Eyes agape, tongue protruding, the light of life lost, staring, sightlessly, searching and finding nothing.

The future is across in front of us. I am not too much of a man to admit that it scares me. I can see the rickety rope bridge swaying gently in the slight breeze. The thick ropes covered in a hanging moss. Half rotten wooden boards, some hanging loosely. They have to support my weight; they have to support my heart.

Is that a shadowy silhouette up ahead? Is it a bridge keeper, a toll collector? What will his questions be? I doubt the accounting he will call for will be as simple as "what is your name?", "What is your quest?", "What is your favourite colour?", or the price he demands as little as $4.75.

Does she wait on the other side? Waiting for our love to find a way? Or like a shade, a spectre does she shimmer in and out of existence. An apparition, not real at all, another false love, a lied love? Will I get to the other side and find her?

Eyes downcast, feet shuffling in the sand, one hand behind my back.

"Hi" is all I can say shyly as I look up at her.

"Hi" she says back.

A single tear begins to pool in the corner of my eye as I slowly bring my hand out from behind my back. Her hazel eyes reflected within the single stone, momentarily creating the perfect gem. Her smile slowly begins to crack on her face.

"Yes!"

She leaps into my arms and before I can even smile, her lips press against mine.

Maybe? I am not a seer. I must trust in the future by taking care of today. Come on! Let's go! You've come this far Dear Reader, let's pay the toll and one foot in front of the other, test the strength of the boards, trust they will get us to where we need to be.

"Come on!", "Let's go!" it may be easier if we close our eyes. Take a chance with me. Here, here is my hand, hold it and we will get there together.

# 58

See I told you, we made it didn't we? Safely on this side I feel comfortable telling you now that it really was touch and go for a minute there. I faltered, I slipped and when that board gave out just near the end there I figured we were done for. Reaching this side I didn't know whether to kiss the ground or just hug you Dear Reader. Well we did it, here we are.

Look over there.

Do you see that truck door opening? She is about to get out and we will meet her for the first time.

Are you holding your breath? You are aren't you, well breathe I don't need you passing out at this point.

There she is! Over there standing on the deck.

See I told you she was beautiful. Oh come on now, stop staring you are making it so obvious. I understand though what a gorgeous creature. Although in fairness that day I didn't think so.

See the grouchy face man standing off to the side with his arms crossed. Yes, yes he is handsome, ha-ha, that's me and I didn't want to have anything to do with her that day.

What's that? Oh yes Dear Reader that little bundle of fluff in her arms, yes that is Artan.

I was more interested in the ball of fluff than the person who placed him in my arms. I really should be embarrassed by the way I treated her those first few days.

Can you remember Dear Reader all the way back to page one when I said that I was a bit of a perfectionist? I had spent my life in search of perfection and a perfect love, by this point I was sure it didn't exist.

I believed that I came close, in the moment when I came to full draw on a bear. Peering through my peep sight, heart racing, locking in like a laser guidance system. This however was mere precision and not perfection it was lacking that intense emotional response. As I see you staring and the memory fully forms, I realize in her I had found a beauty that was so close to perfection for me that I was able to convince myself that my task was complete.

Our love grew slowly, one evening we finally slipped our guards. We were truly at ease with each other at last, able to share a friendly silence, or to talk for an hour without pause. We slowly began to touch each other, brief seemingly casual contacts of which we were both still intensely aware of. She might reach out and cover the back of my hand with hers to emphasize a point, or brush against me as we poured over photos of the past or fish people. Though she was certainly more agile than I. I would take her elbow and help her into a boat, or over some rocks. I would lean over her to point out a young eagle or some fresh bear sign. Love grew slowly but it grew.

"Well I need you" I said. "I think about you all the time and when I imagine my future it all seems better with you by my side", "I really love you". I felt like such an imbecile uttering those banal words. The vocabulary of love so tired and used up. We needed a new word to describe the joy, the renewal, the peace and the love she had brought to my life. Fleebersnick perhaps? Telling her, finally admitting that I loved her; the penultimate experience of my life.

I held her and looked deeply into her eyes "they are pretty"

"What are?"

"Your eyes."

"Ya I am so sure, I look just radiant right now, but I do appreciate the sweet talk UGH! Dork!"

"It's not just sweet talk I can see our future when I stare into their depths. Stay with me a moment longer the night is so beautiful"

"Ok".

"With you I am so happy that it frightens me."

"What?"

"So much happiness cannot go on forever."

When I turned to her and said "I love you". I was amazed to find that, what I had just said was absolutely true.

"I really and truly love you" I said again. "I didn't realize how much until this moment, I didn't know it would be like this" I whispered. "I have thought about you and us constantly since your lips first touched mine. I feel like I have fallen through a black hole in my soul, into a beautiful world that is hinted at in your eyes and I never want to go back again."

"Oh jeez, I love you too, dork!"

I thought I would have so much more to tell you Dear Reader, I don't the day to day falling in love, and the reasons she makes me strive to be a better man. Those moments are ours.

See I sit here on this beach and I watch the sun go down over the ocean, because I love her and time circumstance, other people, rumour and innuendo, and a zombie apocalypse can't change love.

I wish to paraphrase Freddie Mercury here "I'm just the pieces of the man I used to be. I feel like no one told the truth to me about growing up and what a struggle it would be. Just one year of love is better than a lifetime alone. Who wants to live forever when love must die but too much love will kill you in the end."

So here we are Dear Reader, now we have reached the end. Since the outcome is uncertain and in homage to those read books by the light of an alarm clock. I am going to let you Dear Reader choose. Choose your own adventure. You stayed through to here you pick your ending.

Likely- Chapter 4- paragraph 5
Unhappy- Chapter 55- paragraph 13
Happy- Chapter 57- paragraph 6

## The End

# Epilogue

Welcome back. I know, I know, your choice is made and the tale is told. With your decision you have decided how this story ends. I know not how you chose.

I've just been sitting here looking up at the vastness above marvelling at each twinkling star as my fire turns to embers. My mind must be going but the soft glow of my pipe illuminates all the spirits that have come here to join me.

Mom and Dad sit side by side; mom has a smile on her face that I haven't seen in years. I tip my imaginary hat to the pretty young girl sitting next to Uncle Larry. She could only be Annabelle. Is that...... yep Ian is chasing Marie down the beach trying to pinch her ass. OH jeez..... Watch out! that young boy they almost tripped over tracing letters in the sand with a stick could only be Sharpie. Tanya, Chantelle and Christine all sit together, no doubt comparing notes. There is a rowdy ruckus and the simultaneous openings of many beers signal that the Maryland Mafia has arrived. Some others that you don't know but that I love nonetheless have joined the gathering. In fact Fred is talking with Nigel and Walker. Over there is Will, Marc, Norm, Angela, Terri-Lynne and Matt, they are helping Sebastian it is really hard to drink beer with half of a head. It looks like Mellissa is over in the tree line, sullen and angry. Come over I forgive you whether you forgive me or not. A multitude of laughter and a gaggle of foster kids joins my ex wife as she gets close I want to tell her that she deserved much better than she got from me. Oh hi, you must be Destiny, I recognize you from the photos. It is truly a pleasure please sit next to me while I tell this one last tale.

The time has come the gangs all here. I will try to answer the one question I am sure everyone shares. The same question that I asked Larry 20 years ago.

WHY?

I slipped you see, as simple as that, I lost my footing. When I looked back at her, her face was upturned and it seemed to glow under the framing sunlight and light perspiration. I was seized by an almost overwhelming urge to take her into my arms and kiss those moistly parted lips. Instead I turned away and started down the trail.

I dared not look back at her until I had myself fully under control. I could hear her quick light tread on the rocks behind me. We walked on in silence, and I was so preoccupied that I was unprepared for the old root that tangled up my feet.

She tried to break my fall and when I looked back, well if someone were to ask me now what the woman before me (really behind me) looked like? What would I say? Was she tall or short? Were her breasts large or small? Were her hands, her feet graceful? Was her voice melodious? I couldn't say. I had just looked at her but I had not gotten past her eyes. Those big pooling, melting, gorgeous eyes of hers. Eyes that could say more with a glance than any 5 women I had ever known could say with their voices, their bodies, anything. WOW! All I can remember is that there was a message in those eyes for me. How had life hurt her so? Was there anything that I could do? I could not refuse those eyes, my thoughts a hopeless tangle.

I knew in that moment that there was something about her......I had never felt anything like this before, not even in my youth. This feeling inside me for her I cannot describe. If I had of gone to a fortune teller he would have pocketed my money, looked at the moon-struck expression on my face, wink at his assistant and found some pattern in the stars, real or imagined, that would tell me the gods had destined her to be mine for the rest of my life and perhaps for whatever life lies out there beyond death.

I suddenly found myself a man with a future of sorts. I suddenly found I wanted her to spend it with me. Her eyes have been before me every step I have taken since that day.

I can imagine now her head resting on my chest. She is anticipating the deep vibration as I say

I LOVE YOU

Ps. I think I love you is a great ending, most people have not had that in their lives. They have lived life with compromise where loved was concerned. With a mate who was better than nothing but less than everything. She was so much more than that. She may not have been the first woman that I said I love you too. She was the first I was afraid to lose and that I knew my life would be empty without. So even if it was all for nothing, the cost extremely high at least I can say and mean

I LOVE YOU.

# Afterword

The initial draft of this novel was finished May 23 2013 and consisted of 2000 handwritten pages. Today is December 29 2013. Through 4 painstaking rewrites, reviewers' recommendations and editing, copy editing, formatting and numerous other thing you don't think of when you start putting a pencil to paper, you end up with the book that you have just finished. I have thanked those who I needed to in the Authors Note so I won't rehash that here. I will however stress that any errors are mine alone. Editing and grammatical errors have been left in place to help convey the theme of a found manuscript. The professionals at Northern Phoenix are in no way reflected by this choice. Also I want to stress that the novel does not accurately reflect real life events, multiple events have been combined into one to improve readability and the characters in this novel in no way reflect real to life individuals. The people depicted in this fictional tale should be able to recognize themselves in the events, and they and I are the ones who know the truth behind what really happened. That being said I have endeavoured to remain true to the feelings. Zombies are also not real; except perhaps a certain zombie turtle. On my dedication page I simply wrote. May you find out something that you didn't know? I hope in that I was successful. I would like to take the time here to recognize the real players in this tale and a few who though; not in this tale have impacted me positively and their loss I still feel. In no particular order.

> Ralph Steele
>
> Larry Sward
>
> Leona McGahey
>
> Pat Brett
>
> Prof. Janusz K. Zawodny
>
> Steven Crockford
>
> Betty Lessard
>
> Marie Seymour
>
> Rev. Ken Rentz
>
> Erin Hughes
>
> Darcy Weaver

Thank you all.

# Authors Note

It is my wish for you, the real Dear Reader that you enjoy reading this book as much as I enjoyed writing it. Many people go into the making of a life, just as many people go into the making of a book. There are too many people to thank here lest I double the length of this novel. A few notables include my Parents, Uncle Larry, Ian, Betty, Marc, Sebastian, Will, Fred, Matt, and the Maryland Mafia. Shawn Walker for the twice over way that he does things. Terri Lynne for her patience. Destiny knows why. Jon for your counsel, and encouraging letters, through the darkest of times they were a light for me. Brandon, Jody, Tommy, Henry, Matt, Kayti, Tina, and Shyanne for more things than I can list here. Charlotte for your patience in editing and of course the very real loves who inspired this tale. To the folks at Northern Phoenix I am not easy to work with, some grammatical and editorial errors have been left in place to purposely reflect the theme of a found manuscript and in no way represent the editorial staff of Northern Phoenix Press. Though some events in this book may mirror real life occurrences, I have often taken artistic licence; this book is entirely a product of my imagination. Enjoy and may you find out something that you did not know. Proverbs 4:23: Guard your heart above all else, for it determines the course of your life.